Splintered Promises

His Warriors Book 7

By

Ronna M. Bacon

Numbers 23:19
God is not man, that he should lie, or a son of man, that he should change his mind. Has he said, and will he not do it? Or has he spoken, and will he not fulfill it?

Table of Contents

She fought through the darkness that threatened to overcome her and shut her down again. She crawled on hands and knees towards where she thought the door was, scratching her way up the wood to the handle. She stopped, catching her breath, and listening. She hadn't heard anyone around in the building for what she thought was days. She knew she had been in that building for months. She knew who had put her there, who kept coming back asking for something she didn't have.

A sob caught in her throat as she struggled to her feet. The one she loved must have given up on her by now. How would she ever explain what had happened to her?

She twisted at the knob, pulling the door towards her, and staggering out of the room, down the hall, down the stairs, clutching at the handrail to keep herself upright. She shoved at the front door, then pulled it towards, the bright light hurting her eyes, bringing her dirty, scratched hand up to block it.

She couldn't catch her balance as she walked across the broken, sagging boards of the porch and fell down the three steps to the cracked concrete of the walk. She picked herself up, not noticing the new scrapes and bruises. She brought her face up and looked around, her eyes blurring. She staggered once more as she took her steps towards freedom and safety. She had no idea where she was or where she was heading. She just knew she had to get away from that house.

She didn't see the man standing watching her, his golden hair reflecting back the sunlight that had blinded her. He watched her take her steps to freedom, then moved away from the tree he was leaning again, his steps slow and steady as he followed her, watchful for danger that might present itself.

Chapter 1

*A*dam Cavanaugh shoved the heavy toolbox into the bed of his truck and then slammed the tailgate shut. He was exhausted, working construction did that to him, but he promised a friend and his friend's wife he would be at a concert with them tonight. He glanced at the sky. Still sunny and just right for outdoor venue. He sighed, knowing he needed to change his attitude but not sure that he really wanted to be there that night. Anything and everything that could go wrong today had. Sometimes, he wished he had chosen a different line of work.

He turned as he heard tires on the gravel surrounding the new-home build he was working on. At this time of day, nobody should be here. He watched as the luxury car with the heavily tinted windows pulled to a stop behind his truck and waited as the occupants just sat there before one of the windows lowered.

"Hey! You! Yeah, you!" The harsh voice sounded loud in the quiet of the afternoon.

Adam waited, his eyes watchful, not moving from where he leaned against his truck, his hands in his pocket, keys in one hand.

"Hey, you! You deaf? I want to talk to you." The voice sounded angry.

"You're trespassing, in case you didn't know." Adam finally responded, his baritone voice a sharp contrast to the nasal tones of the man yelling at him.

"I want to talk to you."

"Then, talk. I'm not stopping you."

Adam watched as the back door of the car opened, and a heavyset man appeared and then approached him. Now, what, he thought. He didn't move, just waited. The man stood in front of him for a moment, then reached for Adam's arm. Adam ducked and moved backwards to the front of his vehicle, his fingers clicking the lock button on the key fob. If he could make it in there, he'd be safe and could call for help.

His eyes on the man in front of him, he didn't see the second man approaching from his other side until he felt the round metal of a gun muzzle against his back stop his movements. He froze, his one hand still jammed in his pocket, one hand reached for his truck door, and waited.

His arms were grabbed in a tight hold and he was forcibly walked to the vehicle. He struggled but couldn't get his arms loose.

"What exactly do you want?" His voice was calm, even though his heart was racing.

"This house? I want it torn down."

"Not happening. As far as I know, everything is legal and above board." He strained to see the man talking to him, but the tinted window wasn't down low enough for him to see anything other than a dark shape.

"No. You tear it down and don't build here."

He didn't see the fist headed his way until too late. His head shot back and he would have staggered except for the tight hold the one man had on his arms. He struggled but couldn't get loose. He watched in horror as the first man opened the trunk and removed a gas can before heading towards the house. Adam wrenched his way free, his steel-toed boot hitting the man holding him in his knee and sending him to the ground. He flew across the uneven ground and launched himself at the man as he set the gas can down. The man grunted as he fell under Adam's assault before he shrugged Adam off and turned on him, his feet and fists leaving Adam in a crumpled broken heap on the ground before he glanced back as his employer, who nodded.

The flames from the house lit up the sky, smoke rising thick and black before it drifted towards town. The light of red and orange flames flickered across Adam's face, even as the sound of the oncoming sirens rose and fell.

Josiah Silverthorn hit the brakes of his truck and slid to a stop, his eyes on the fire ahead of him. Where was his friend? He had been worried when Adam hadn't shown up or returned any of his text messages. His cousin, Catriona McGill, stared at the fire, then at Josiah.

"Josiah, is this where your friend was working today?" Shock filled her hazel eyes, even as she pulled at her dark auburn pony tail.

"It is. Come on. Let's see if he's around anywhere. I know he really didn't want to be at the concert, but he would have come, just to keep his word."

Josiah and Catriona walked towards the police line, their eyes searching. Josiah stopped and pulled Catriona to one side as a team of paramedics rushed by them.

"I don't like this, Catriona." Josiah was stopped by a patrol officer. "That's Adam's truck. Now, where is he?"

"There. Is that him the paramedics are working on?" Catriona pointed, knowing full well that it likely was her cousin's friend.

"Oh, no! I think it is!" He spun, searching for someone he could talk to.

The paramedics pushed the stretcher towards them and the two stepped to the side, their eyes on the figure lying on the stretcher. They turned and followed, Catriona drawing close as she studied the man lying there, battered and bruised, blood staining the copper of his hair and the dark brown of his neatly trimmed beard.

The senior paramedic, Ezra, shot her a look, then shared one with Josiah, shaking his head.

Adam stirred, groaning as he did so, his eyelids flickering as he turned and tried to rise. He fought against the restraints holding him and against the hands of the two paramedics, arms and legs twitching, hands flailing. Without thinking, Catriona moved forward and caught his hand. His hand turned and gripped hers tight enough to hurt and he stilled.

His eyes flickered open and stayed open long enough for her to see the dark brown of them. He mumbled something and she leaned forward.

"You? You're here? Don't leave me." His voice was barely above a whisper. His eyes slid shut once more and he lay still.

Catriona tried to pull her hand free and couldn't break the grip it was held with. She spun as best she could to look at Josiah, who merely shrugged, a half-smile on his face.

"I would say you're going with him." Josiah shook his head even as a small grin twitched at his lips. "Ezra, I guess she's riding with you."

"That's what I would say. Until we know for sure how bad it is, I don't want to risk prying his fingers loose from hers. John, all set?" At his partner's nod, Ezra pointed at Catriona. "Walk towards the rig. When we get there, we'll be lowering the stretcher so we can load it. Just move with us. Josiah, we'll need you to help your cousin in."

Josiah nodded, watching as they loaded the stretcher, Catriona's gaze finding his, worry and something else he couldn't quite read in her eyes. He stood as the ambulance pulled away before turning to see who he could talk to.

Chapter 2

*J*osiah stood in the hallway outside the cubicle Adam lay in and watched as the physician and the nurses worked around him. Catriona still stood at his side, unable to extract her hand from his. Josiah frowned, not quite sure what was going on before he turned as he heard footsteps heading his way.

Andrew McBeth, police chief for their town and a close friend, stood beside him for a moment, a questioning look on his face as he studied Catriona.

"What's up with that?" He nodded towards her.

"I have no idea. She took his hand when he was fighting Ezra and John and he won't let go of it."

"Interesting. That's our Adam doing that?" Andrew shook his head even as he moved towards the exam room. Adam was known for treating ladies with care and this was out of character for him.

"Doc?"

The physician turned as he heard Andrew behind him. "Andrew? What brings you here? I thought it would be one of your detectives."

"Bill Buckley's on his way. I was here anyway, visiting someone from church, and stopped by. How is he?"

"We're still assessing him, but we really need him to let go on this lady's hand, and he won't."

"Let me see what I can do." Andrew approached Catriona.

"Catriona, can you move your hand if I can get his fingers loosened at bit?"

She nodded. "I hope I can and that I still have feeling in them. He's got a tight grip, you know?"

"Working construction will do that. Let's see how we manage." Andrew gave her a quick grin.

Andrew was finally able to free Catriona's hand and caught her by the arm as she stumbled backwards.

"Here, take it easy. Josiah's out in the hall. Let's get you out there. How's your hand?"

Catriona stared at it, a frown in place, not quite sure what had happened. "It's fine, I think." She turned to look back at Adam, taking in the bruises and cuts on his face and arms that she could see. "They really beat him up, didn't they? What was the purpose of it all?"

Andrew shrugged as, hand on her elbow, he moved her from the room and towards the waiting room. "Let's go out here and sit. Josiah has some water for you, I think."

Josiah sat down beside her cousin, after offering her the bottle of water. She drank, then turned to him.

"You should be at home. Faith needs you with your sick little one."

"He's not sick, Catriona. He's teething and not a happy camper with that. I talked to her. She's fine with me here." He searched his cousin's face, frown in place, as he tried to work out what had happened.

"What happened tonight, Catriona?" He waited as she sat and stared at the door to the examination rooms. "Adam seemed to know you."

She finally laid her head back and closed her eyes, fatigue showing in the circles under her eyes and the paleness of her face. It wasn't just tonight that caused that, she knew. She hadn't been sleeping, the past making it impossible to do just that. She finally spoke, her voice low.

"I know Adam from college."

"You what?" Josiah turned to her, not quite believing what she had said.

"I know him from college. We dated almost from the time we met there our first year."

"And you never ever said a word!" He spun in his seat to stare towards the rooms. "And Adam didn't either."

"No, he wouldn't. He's too much of a gentleman. We didn't tell you. There's a lot of reasons why."

"Your brother for one, I would think. Did Carey really think he had that much influence over your life?"

She nodded. "He did." She bit her lip, not quite sure how to proceed, then sighed, knowing what she was about to say would come out anyway at some point, after what had just happened. She reached for the necklace around her neck and pulled it out, the emerald stone in the ring sparkling in the light. "Adam gave me this. We were to be married, Josiah. We had it all planned. Mom was working with us on it as was Adam's Mom."

"What happened?" Josiah's eyes studied his cousin's face, seeing the sadness lined there.

"Carey. He found out and locked me away where no one could find me. He kept me there for months."

"I wondered where you were. Adam couldn't find you?"

She shook her head. "No one could. I finally convinced him that I wasn't going to marry Adam. I know I hurt Adam so much, but Carey threatened his life."

"Catriona, you should have told us. We could have dealt with him."

"Yeah, well, you really didn't know him. You have no idea what he's capable of or what kind of friends he has." She sighed. "I knew coming here to live would be difficult. I just didn't imagine how much."

Josiah's arm went around her and he hugged her. "So that's what he meant." At her nod, he continued. "Well, then, as his fiancee I get you get to stay and see him then. Put the ring on your finger." She stared at him, shaking her head. "No, put it on. That gives you the right to be with him. Adam's parents are on the way in. Talk to them. I know they didn't understand what happened, but they'll support you. They've missed you so much."

"I can't, Josiah. Not after what I did. I can't face him either." She was up out of her chair and running from the room, almost running into the couple entering.

The woman stopped, staring after her, calling her name. The man looked the direction she had run and then shook his head, his arm around the woman's shoulders as he drew her into the waiting room and towards the clerk's desk. A few words and they headed down the hall.

"Adam's parents. They got here fast." Andrew nodded towards them.

"They were in town. They weren't supposed to be. They have something on this weekend but for the life of me, I can't think what." Josiah's brow furrowed.

"Was your cousin serious, Josiah?" Andrew was having trouble figuring that one out, knowing Adam.

"I think she was, Andrew. She wouldn't say something like that if it wasn't."

"Do we need to look for her brother?"

"Maybe, but I'm not even sure where he is now. They haven't talked about him in five, maybe six years. He was wild, always was. Mom and Dad suspected he was into drug dealing and crime."

Thirty-six hours later, Adam finally managed to crack his eyes open and keep them that way. Everything was still blurry, though, and he blinked, trying to bring the room to focus. He frowned as he looked around. A hospital room? How did that happen? The last thing he remembered was walking away from his girlfriend's apartment.

He heard movement to his right and turned his head, his eyes closing at the pain that shot through it.

"Adam? Can you open your eyes again, Adam?" The voice was familiar.

"Mom? What are you doing here? Aren't you supposed to be at home?" Adam grimaced as the light hit his eyes.

"We are home, Adam. You're in our hospital."

He felt his mother's hand on his forehead, even the light touch hurting. "Mom, what happened? Don't I have class today?"

His mother, Hannah, stared at him. "What are you talking about, Adam?"

"What day is it? And where's Catriona? Isn't she here?"

Hannah turned to stare at the nurse. "What's wrong with him, nurse?"

"I'll be right back, Mrs. Cavanaugh. I just need to call the doctor. He wanted to know when Adam woke up. Don't worry. We'll figure it out."

Jonathan Cavanaugh stood behind his wife, his eyes on his son. "He's lost some time there, Hannah. A few years by the sounds of it. He doesn't know about Catriona."

She shook her head. "No, he doesn't. We need to get her here. Can you find her?"

Jonathan shrugged. "I can try but I can't make her come if she doesn't want to, you know."

"Please try, dear. I'll pray that her heart is still open enough to him to come to the hospital. I don't know what happened to them, Jonathan."

"I don't know either, Hannah, but maybe this is God's way of bringing them back together. Let me see what I can do."

❖ ❖ ❖ ❖ ❖

Answering the ring at her doorbell, Catriona stood and stared at the man standing there. What was he doing here? Was Adam worse?

"Jonathan? What are you doing here? Is it Adam?" Her eyes widened in fright, then she recovered quickly to hide her emotions.

Jonathan studied the woman standing in front of him, his thoughts going back years to when he first met her, thinking that his son and this young woman were so suited to one another. Adam had never said much about what had happened to the two of them. Catriona just disappeared from his life.

"No, he's awake. He's asking for you."

"For me? That can't be right. We haven't talked or seen each other in years."

"No, you haven't, but it's true. He wants to see you." Jonathan hesitated, his eyes dropping the hand holding his keys. "The thing of it is, Catriona. He doesn't remember much. He thinks you're still together and you're back in college."

"What? How can that be?" She stepped back from the door. "I'm sorry. Come in. Now explain."

Jonathan stopped just inside the door, his eyes assessing the young woman standing in front of him. "The beating he took? The doctors warned about a concussion. But they didn't warn us that he'd have amnesia."

"Amnesia? I thought that only happened in books."

Jonathan shook his head. "No. Hannah called me on the way over here. The doctor says he can't remember much past the last few days of college. He's asking for you, Catriona? Can you come?"

She blew a breath, then turned and paced. "You have no idea what you're asking of me, Jonathan."

"Look. Hannah and I, well, we thought of you as the daughter God didn't bless us with. I don't know what happened to break you two up, but please? Can you come? Even for one visit."

She shook her head. "I can't, Jonathan. I just can't." She stopped, her back to him, rigid and straight. "I just can't go near him."

Jonathan walked towards her, laying a hand on her shoulder. "Please, Catriona?"

She finally nodded. "Just one visit, Jonathan. That's all I can do. I'll meet you there."

He nodded and walked back to his car, waiting for her to leave. Catriona pulled out in front of him, not seeing the car that had parked across the street from her house, that pulled away and followed them.

She hesitated at the room door, not sure what she would find. She remembered his words from the other day, but knew he wouldn't want to be around her if he knew just how dangerous it was for him.

Jonathan's hand came down on her shoulder and he squeezed it.

"Come on, love. Let's go see Adam."

Catriona's feet propelled her slowly across the floor until she stood at the end of the bed, her eyes on Adam. She didn't see Hannah standing there or Jonathan moving to wrap his arm around his wife. Adam slept, but she could see the ravages of what he had been through on his face.

Lord, I'm here but I know I shouldn't be. I prayed we'd not have contact living in the same town, but it looks as if we will. I can't go through this any more. I need to leave this in the past.

Adam's head moved restlessly as his eyes flickered open. He blinked, then focused on the woman standing watching him.

"Catriona? You're here? What? Where am I?" His head moved restlessly as he searched the room, his hand plucking at the blanket.

His mother moved forward to lay a hand on his arm, stilling his motions and causing him to look at her.

"Mom? Aren't you supposed to be at home? What are you doing here? Dad, you too?" His restless movements continued, and Hannah shot a look at Catriona.

Catriona moved to the side of the bed, her hand coming to rest on Adam's shoulder.

"Adam, I think the doctors want you to lie still."

He laid back, his eyes on her. "Where were you? Did your class run late?"

She shook her head, willing the tears from her eyes. She couldn't do this. She would wait until he was asleep and then leave. She watched as his eyes slid closed and his body relaxed, then turned and walked from the room, Adam's parents staring after her.

"Jonathan? Go after her."

"Won't do any good, Hannah. She said she'd only make one visit here, and this was it. Did Adam ever say what happened?"

She shook her head as her eyes traced her son's face. "Not a word, Jonathan, in all those years."

He nodded, before turning to look at the door. "She's walked away again, Hannah. We've got it to go through all over with Adam."

She didn't say anything. Then she spoke. "This time, we leave it with God, dear. God will work it out."

Josiah looked up as his cousin walked towards him, discouragement in her demeanour. He frowned. She had called, asked him to meet her and then had been late showing up. That wasn't like her, and her stance wasn't like her at all.

"Thanks, Josiah." She accepted the cup of tea he handed her, settling beside him on the park bench. She didn't say a word for a long time.

"Catriona, you okay?"

She shook her head. "I really don't know, Josiah. Jonathan came and got me to go see Adam."

"I bet that went over well." Josiah was defensive of his cousin, even though Adam was a close friend, one of a group of eight from college.

"I went and saw him, Josiah. I said I'd make one visit only." She was quiet for a moment, then spoke again. "He thinks we're still a couple, Josiah. He doesn't realize we split up. He doesn't remember anything past the last part of our last year at college."

"What? How?" Josiah stared at her, his mouth opening and closing before a grimness set into his face. "Amnesia?"

She nodded and then swiped at the tears on her face. "How do I stay in this town, Josiah?   How do I face everyone at church? Your friends?"

Josiah heaved a sigh, then sat in silence, his mind racing, his heart in prayer. "Are you going back to see him?"

She shook her head. "Not unless I'm forced to. There's no point, Josiah. There's nothing there."   She sat, her hands folded around the takeout cup of tea, a blank look on her face.

Josiah studied her.   How would she survive in this town, given this?   He knew Adam well enough to know that he wouldn't let it rest and to go through the break up again is not what he wanted either one of them to go through. He could tell there was something still there. He knew her well. If there hadn't been, she would have already returned her ring.

"Pray about it, cuz. Talk to Silas too. Don't close it off completely. With your line of work and his, you're going to cross paths at some point.   Decide now how you're going to handle it. Avoiding it won't work."

She shook her head. "I don't know, Josiah. I really don't know. Did you find out why this happened to him?"

He shook his head. "Andrew or Bill are not saying. I've talked to the guys. They think he was ambushed and then the house burnt, but they don't know for sure. I haven't talked to Jason Long yet. He might know more."

"It's sad, Josiah. All that work." She sighed. "I would have met Adam at some point on that build. The couple talked to me about doing the interior for them."

Josiah nodded. "I pray that it was just a one-time thing, what happened."

She spun to look at him, her cold tea splashing over her hand and she absentmindedly wiped it on her jeans. "You think it might not be?"

He shrugged. "With what Faith and I went through and what our other friends went through, I have my doubts."

She turned once more to look out over the stormy lake. "It's going to storm, Josiah. I hope that's not a sign of what we're facing."

Josiah nodded, praying they wouldn't, but knowing full well that's where this couple was headed. Please, dear Lord, protect them. Protect their hearts. Catriona has trouble with Your promises, with people not keeping promises they've made to her. Help her to trust.

Chapter 3

*A*dam groaned as his father helped him up the stairs to his place. He never realized how hard it was to climb stairs. After spending five days in the hospital, he was glad to be home again. He had talked to the contractor of the home build and knew it would be months before they'd be ready for him to tackle the interior trim and finishing again. Tom, the contractor, had been concerned when he heard the extent of Adam's injuries. He sighed, nodding to his father as he sank gratefully into his easy chair. The cracked ribs and the hairline fracture in his left arm would take time to heal.

"Can I get you anything, Adam?" His father was worried. Adam had insisted he come to his own home, even though he didn't remember it.

"Are you sure this is my home, Dad? I don't remember it at all." Adam looked around at the comfortably furnished room.

"It is, son. You did the restoration on it. The local paper featured it and you've gotten more work that you can handle." Jonathan sank onto the couch, his eyes on his son, a frown on his face. "Adam, about Catriona."

"Where is she, Dad? I thought she'd have come back to the hospital." He moved restlessly, his head sinking back on the chair. "What happened?"

Jonathan sighed, knowing he would have to break the news to his son, but not quite sure how to. "Let me make us some coffee and then we'll talk." He stood, hesitating for a moment, before his hand touched his son's shoulder as he moved towards the kitchen.

Lord, how do I tell him that they're not a couple? He can't handle that right now. He turned, his eyes on the kitchen doorway, and then sighed. He would be heading back to talk to Catriona, to see what he could work out for her to come and see Adam once more.

Jonathan stood, coffee cups in hand, in the living room, his eyes on his son, a sigh moving through him as a prayer. He stared down at the cups, before heading back to the kitchen to dump them out and turn off the coffee pot. Adam was sleeping, as he well needed, and Jonathan reached for the green and white afghan to spread over his son. He stood, a hesitant look on his face, before he nodded and headed for the door. Adam would tell him not to hover over him, and Jonathan had to agree. He knew Hannah would be heading this way shortly.

Catriona moved restlessly through her showroom, straightening brochures and sample books. She had had a busy morning, garnering more work that she could almost handle. She sighed. She knew she would soon have to hire someone to run the office, and she wasn't quite sure she wanted to give that up. It would take the right person to step in, she knew.

She headed for her office and the cup of tea she had made, how many hours ago she couldn't remember.

She slid the folder from the house that had burned in front of her. It would take months before it would be ready for her to walk in and do her part of making it a home. She had talked to the homeowners, who were still in shock over what had happened. She hadn't heard anything more about the culprits, but her cousin had assured her the police were working on the case.

She raised her eyes to the large framed photo she had hung on the wall across from her desk. She read the words written there, the promise that God would never leave her. She sighed. She needed that truth today. Having faced Adam twice in a week took a toll on her. She sat back, eyes thoughtful, her heart in prayer, before she heard the buzzer that sounded when the front door opened. She rose, hesitation in her movements. Somehow, she knew whoever this was, it would change her life, and not necessarily send her in the way she wanted to go.

She stood for a moment, studying the two young woman who stood there, around her age, she thought.

"Can I help you?"

The two whirled around, startled at her voice.

"Oh, my goodness! I wasn't expecting you to appear so quietly." The taller of the two moved towards her, her hand out. "I don't think we've had a chance to meet. I understand you ran into my husband a few days ago."

Catriona tilted her head as she studied the woman. "I might have."

The woman laughed. "Forgive me. I'm Phoebe McBeth, Andrew's wife. And this is Candace, Jonah's wife. We're friends with your cousin's wife, and our husbands are part of the group of friends that includes Adam."

Catriona nodded as she shook hands with the woman. "What can I do for you, though? Somehow, I don't think you're here to have me decorate your homes."

Phoebe and Candace shared a look.

"That would be nice. You have some beautiful accessories here. I need to go through them." Phoebe turned in a circle. "Andrew's home was nice when we married, but bare and I've been gradually adding some trinkets and doodads, as he calls them. But, you're right. That's not why we're here. Our group of ladies, who includes Faith, meet on a weekly basis on Thursday nights for Bible study. We'd be glad to have you join us."

Catriona took a step back, a wary look on her face. Was this a way of trapping her to meet and face Adam again?

"I'm not sure that I can make it. I've been really busy and have been putting in a lot of hours."

"But you do need some downtime at some point, don't you?" Candace spoke up. "I know I do. We won't push you. We just wanted to ask you. Faith was going to but she didn't want to, in case you resented her asking."

"Faith said that? She should know better. Josiah's like a brother to me." Catriona bit off her words, her thoughts going to her own brother. Where was he now and how much had he been following her? Someone had, and she was sure it was Carey.

"No pressure. We share hostessing duties. This week, we're at Jonah and Candace's, out on their farm." Phoebe watched the shadows crossing Catriona's face and wondered just what was going on with her. Andrew had mentioned what had happened with Adam, and her thoughts went to these two. How close were they, actually?

They spoke for a few more minutes before Catriona needed to take a call. Phoebe and Candace walked away, their hearts burdened for this young woman.

Catriona set her phone down. She had been thankful for the call. She wasn't ready yet to join in a group of woman. She didn't know that she ever would be. She was uncomfortable around people she didn't know. And she could thank her brother for that. She tamped down the anger she felt towards him, knowing that if she gave in to it, it would destroy her.

She sighed to herself as she saw the man walking towards her. She couldn't lock the door, it was too early in the day. She watched as he entered and then just stood, his manner hesitant as if he wasn't quite sure he should be there.

"Jonathan? Can I help you with something?" Her eyes never left the face so much like his son's.

He finally nodded. "I hope you'll reconsider what you told me, when I asked you to come and see Adam in the hospital." He looked down, tracing a pattern in the floor with the toe of his shoe. He would beg, if he had to. Adam's health was too important.

She shook her head. "I can't, Jonathan. It's over between us, has been for years."

"The thing is, Catriona, is that Adam doesn't remember that. All he knows is that the woman he loves isn't coming near him, and that hurts him in a way I don't want to see."

Catriona crossed her arms across her waist and paced, stopping in front of the windows to stare out. Her brows drew together as she stared at the car parked across the road from her business, just sitting there. She realized it wasn't the first time she had seen it. It seemed to be following her, though why, she had no idea.

"I know what you're asking, Jonathan. But I can't."

"Hannah and I, we never knew what happened. Never questioned Adam. Maybe if we had, we wouldn't have to have this conversation. He has never said any against you, Catriona. Even in his deepest hurt, he wouldn't let anyone say bad about you. He loves you deeply, deeply enough that he has never moved on."

Catriona stiffened. "He has to have, Jonathan. I have."

"Have you? Somehow, I don't think you have. What was it that happened?"

She shook her head, willing the tears she so wanted to shed back down, and turned to face him. "I can't say, Jonathan. Why do you think I need to see Adam? Surely he has friends and family that can help."

Jonathan nodded at that. "He does, but they're not you. You're the one he wants to see."

She sighed. "Jonathan, I can't do this. It's just impossible."

He studied for a moment, before nodding, disappointment on his face. "That's okay. I just thought I'd ask. Adam still doesn't remember anything past college. That's a long time to lose, Catriona. I just thought…". His voice died away as he turned and walked out of the building and back to his car.

She watched him walk away, her hands on her face, distress in her eyes. She reached to finger the ring she wore every day. Adam had refused to take it back, stating that God meant for them to be together and that someday they would be. He loved her too much to give up on her. She had not seen him since her captivity until that moment at the build site. She had had to work for the past few days to tamp down any feelings she had for him.

She turned, reaching for her phone as it chimed. She frowned at the message, then froze. Carey had found her number, had found her. She was no longer safe. She spun in a circle, knowing she couldn't leave as she had clients coming in. But this changed everything. She would need to see Adam, to warn him.

Adam rose from his chair, waiting until he felt steady on his feet, and made his way to the bedroom. He needed to shower and get cleaned up, but he wasn't sure if he'd able to. He turned slowly as he heard the doorbell and sighed. He walked towards the door, his hand running along the wall to steady himself.

He opened the door, to stand staring at the woman standing in front of him. He reached for her and she stepped back.

"Catriona? You're here? Come in." He waited, his brows drawn down, not quite sure of what was happening.

"Adam?"   She stepped inside and stood, her hands rubbing up and down her arms, a look in her face he had never seen before. "Can we talk?"

He nodded, his movements slow and jerky and pointed to the living room.

She stared around and then turned to him, a sigh heaving through her body. This was just so hard.   Lord, why am I here, anyway?

"Catriona?"   Adam's voice pulled her out of her thoughts and she looked up at him.

"Adam."   She paused, not quite sure on the words. "How are you feeling?"

He shrugged, and then grimaced at the pull on his ribs. "I've been better. But that's not why you're here, is it?"

She shook her head.   "Your Dad say you have amnesia? Is that correct?"

"That's what I'm told.   I don't remember." He watched her face, seeing the emotions flickering across it. "Why?"

She rubbed her hands along her legs. "This is so hard, Adam. I don't know how to say it." She pulled the necklace from her neck and unfastened it, setting the ring on the table between them. "We're not together any more.   We broke up just as college finished."

"No. That's not right. We planned to marry. How can you say that?" He leaned forward, forgetting how battered his body was.

She nodded and then rose. "It's true, Adam. We did break up. You refused to take the ring back." She walked towards the door, hearing his protests behind her. She shook her head, not looking at him. "Good bye, Adam. I'm sure we'll run into each other over the next few weeks. I'll be wrapping up my business and moving on to a different town."

He stood in the doorway, watching as she drove away, his hand clenched around the ring. Something wasn't right, he thought. She wouldn't have done this. He turned, closing the door behind him and headed for his bedroom, falling to his knees in the hallway as sudden, intense pain hit him, his eyes squeezing shut against it. The pain took him into a blackness he didn't think he had ever seen before or would even survive.

Chapter 4

*A*ndrew rang Adam's doorbell, then frowned when Adam didn't answer. He turned to Samuel Harding, another friend of theirs.

"I know he's home. I just spoke with his Dad."

Samuel shrugged. "Sleeping, maybe?" He reached to try the door, surprised that it swung open.

Andrew reached for his weapon and pushed the door all the way open, motioning for Samuel to stay where he was. He entered, eyes searching. He paused beside Adam's still form and then shouted for Samuel to call 911 while he searched the rest of the house, holstering his weapon as he made his way back to Adam.

Samuel knelt beside him. "What happened here, Andrew?"

"I have no idea. His Dad said he was on his own, but I wonder." He knelt, reaching for Adam's hand to unclench it, catching the ring as it fell.

"Where did that come from?" Samuel searched Andrew's face, seeing something there he didn't understand.

"I think I know. There're the paramedics. Go on, let them in, Samuel."

Andrew stood back, watching as Ezra and Tom worked over Adam.

"How is he, Ezra?"

Ezra shrugged as he sat back on his heels. "I really don't know, Andrew. He's unconscious, but I don't see any new injuries."

"That's what I thought. Listen, I'll be in shortly. Samuel, can you ride with him? I'll call his parents. Then I have a stop to make." His grimness startled Samuel for a moment before he nodded agreement and followed the stretcher out of the house.

An hour later, Andrew stood in front of a door in a house across town. He sighed, knowing this would be a very difficult discussion he would have to have. He turned, feeling eyes watching him, but not seeing anyone. Not again, please, dear Lord. I don't think our friends can take this.

He turned as he heard the door open, and Catriona stood in front of him. He could tell she had been crying, the red eyes gave it away as did the soaking wet tissues she held in her hand.

"Is there something I can help you with, Chief?"

He nodded and pointed behind her. "Can I come in? I doubt you'll want your neighbours watching me talk to you on your front porch." He assessed her, but she didn't give away a lot.

She finally stood aside and pointed to the den. "In there, I guess." She perched on the edge of a love seat as he sat across from her, suddenly unsure of his words.

"You went to see Adam today." He watched until she reluctantly nodded. "And you left a ring with him." He held up the ring.

"And how would you be knowing this?"

"Because I unclenched his hand to find it. He collapsed in the hallway of his home, Catriona. And I'm guessing it was shortly after you saw him. Combined with what happened to him a week ago, I have to follow this up. So, tell me. Did you go and see him?"

She finally nodded. "I did. Jonathan asked me to go, to make it right, to be his fiancee again. I can't do that, Andrew. He doesn't remember that we broke up the first time and I can't live through this again."

Andrew nodded. "Did he say anything?"

She shook her head. "Not really. At least, I don't remember." She looked up at him. "And don't ask me to pretend. I can't do it. I'm starting the process of shutting down my business and moving on."

Andrew stared at her. "Running, are you? You won't get far. I know Adam. Once he's given his heart, he won't take it back."

She rose and paced. "He has to. I can't let him cling to a hope that's not there."

"And somehow I think you're protesting too much. What actually happened, Catriona? You're the only one who seems to know."

The shattering of the front window glass sent Andrew flying across the room and tackling Catriona, holding her to the floor even as he pulled out his phone and called it in. She struggled to rise until he shoved her back down and growled at her to lie still.

The responding officers searched but the assailant was long gone. Andrew was frustrated as he returned to the house and found Catriona in her office, her face white, hands clenched as the paramedics assessed her. She shrugged off their concerns and turned to Andrew.

"Didn't find anyone, did you?"

He nodded to the paramedics to leave before he spoke. "No, we didn't, and somehow you knew we wouldn't. I can't have someone going around shooting up my town. You talk to me here and now or I'll take you downtown and lock you up as a material witness." His eyes were hard as he stared at her, muttered as his phone rang.

He listened for a moment, before he turned back to Catriona, his eyes even harder and his face grimmer.

"Catriona, that was Jonathan. They're planning on taking Adam into surgery. He's developed a brain bleed they have to address."

She shook her head, her hands on her mouth. "Dear Lord, not that." Then she began to shake and Andrew reached out to steady her, shoving her into a chair and heading to find water for her.

She took the bottle, rolling it in her hands. "Andrew, I didn't mean to upset him. I didn't mean for this to happen."

"I know you didn't." He crouched down in front of her. "We need you to help us. Can you do that? Just pretend to be his friend if you can't do anything closer." He watched her face, his eyes raising briefly as he nodded at the patrol officer. "But I need you to talk to me. You need to tell me what caused you to break it off from him."

Tears thickened in her throat and she swiped them from her face. "He threatened to kill Adam." She raised her head, looked up, even as she blinked at the tears.

Whatever had happened, Andrew hadn't expected to hear this. He drew a chair close and sat, his eyes on her.

"Who threatened Adam? Catriona, talk to me. You're not making sense."

"I don't know if I can." She abruptly raised her hand and threw the water bottle at the wall. Andrew turned and watched as it fell to roll across the floor. "It's been too hard."

Andrew rose abruptly. "Where are your keys?"

"What?"

"Your keys. Leave them with Ed here. He'll see that your window is boarded up and the doors locked. I'm taking you with me."

He grasped her arm as she resisted.

"No, I can't do that. That puts everyone in danger."

"Catriona. Get your purse. Give Ed your keys. We're leaving." He watched her, a hard look in his eyes. "If you don't come, I'll arrest you."

She stared at him, then turned to find her purse, slapping the extra set of house keys into his hands before stalking from the room.

Andrew handed the keys to Ed, shaking his head at the question there. He then followed her to his car, shutting the door after her, standing staring around, a frown on his face. Who was out there? He knew that feeling all too well and he didn't like it.

As he pulled away from the house, he watched Catriona struggle to control her emotions.

"Talk. Tell me exactly what you haven't told Adam. And when he's well enough, you'll be talking with him."

She shook her head. "I can't."

"You will or I will, but one of us will. It's past time, Catriona. Someone went after him last week and I need to know if it's related to what you went through."

She sighed, her eyes staring out the side window. "I don't know where to start. Adam and I keep our relationship very quiet. We didn't want people to know and talk. Somehow, he found out and kidnapped me, keeping me captive for six months."

"Who, Catriona? You haven't said who yet."

"It's so hard." She swiped at the tears on her face. "My brother, Carey. He was determined that, because no woman would have him, I didn't deserve to have a man in my life. He's sick, Andrew. I haven't seen him since I convinced him that Adam and I were done and that I had given Adam back his ring. He threatened to kill him in front of me. I couldn't let him hurt Adam."

"Did you tell anyone at all?"

She shook her head. "I couldn't. He threatened more than just Adam."

"And where is he now?" Andrew's eyes searched around, looking for danger.

"I don't know." She shrugged. "After I got away, I ran as far as I could. He had disappeared. I don't know if he's alive or dead, and I don't want to know."

Andrew nodded as he pulled into his own driveway. "I'm taking you in to Phoebe. I heard she called on you one day. She'll help you. I'm leaving a patrol car here as well."

"Why, Andrew?"

"Why?" He turned to stare at her as he led her up the sidewalk.

"Why do this?"

"Because Adam's a good friend and he seems to think he loves you. Besides, I don't like to hear what you just told me. You need protection. And, I think you need to hear Phoebe's and my story."

Chapter 5

Andrew walked towards the hospital, across the hot pavement, the heat from it rising in shimmers. He searched the area, feeling something off but now quite sure what it was.

He greeted Jonathan at the door to Adam's room, his eyes searching for his friend.

"How is he, Jonathan?"

Jonathan drew a deep breath. "They didn't do the surgery. They decided to wait but it's touch and go. Andrew, who did this?"

"We're investigating, but with few leads, we're not getting very far. I need to talk to you and Hannah. Is she around?"

"She went to the cafeteria to grab us something to eat." He walked back to his son's bedside, his hand reaching for his son's arm. "What about?"

"I talked to Catriona. I have some news I need to share with you both." Andrew eyed his friend, the whiteness of his face, the slackness of his features. "What are they saying?"

"The bleeding has stopped and they think he'll be okay. He'll need to take it easy for a while though."

Andrew snorted. "They don't know him very well, do they?" He watched as Adam moved restlessly. "He's doing that a lot?"

Jonathan nodded. "We need to get it stopped, but nothing we do helps. They don't want to drug him if they can help it. The only thing that helped was Catriona." He looked up as Andrew sighed.

"Yeah, about her." Andrew turned as Hannah appeared behind him, surprise on her face.

"Andrew? What are you doing here?" She handed the takeout containers to her husband. "I can go get a coffee for you."

He held up his hand. "That's not necessary." He paused, not quite sure how to proceed. He kept his eyes on Adam.

"Hannah, I told Jonathan I had a talk with Catriona." He sighed, biting his lip before he continued. "It wasn't anything that Adam did that split them up. She tells me someone threatened to kill him and any of her friends that intervened. She was kept captive for six months before she was released."

"Who, Andrew? Never mind. I have a good idea." Hannah stared first at her husband, then at her son.

He turned to Hannah. "Who?"

"Her brother. He's a piece of work. I never trusted him."

"Carey. He tried to break us all the time we dated." They all spun to stare at Adam, who had roused during the conversation. The few words had exhausted him.

"Why didn't you say anything, then?" Jonathan moved closer to the bed.

"I didn't have proof of what he had done. When she left me the letter, telling me it was over, I went into shock. I need to see her." Adam drifted off again.

"Her brother? And just where is he now?" Jonathan spun to stare at Andrew.

"We have no idea. He's disappeared, did that when he broke up these two. Listen, I need to run. I'm hoping that Catriona will come by. She's with Phoebe right now."

"With your wife? Okay. That might make a difference."

"Has Adam remembered more past college?" Hannah touched her son's hand. "Andrew, we need Catriona here, now."

He hesitated, knowing that if he brought her to Adam, he could be bringing in a shooter to the hospital. "Let me talk to her again."

"Just get her here, Andrew. Adam needs her."

"I'll do my best. In the meantime, I'm putting an officer at his door around the clock."

✧ ✧ ✧ ✧ ✧

Catriona stared at Phoebe, her cup of tea forgotten in front on her, her mouth slightly open before she snapped it closed. She shook her head.

"There's no way you two went through that!"

Phoebe grinned at her as she nodded. "We did.   Andrew swept in on his motorcycle, swept me away to safety, married me the next day to provide safety and security for me.   It was difficult, Catriona, more difficult than you will ever know. I had been beaten and threatened to the point that I couldn't talk, didn't talk until they went after Andrew.   We survived, stronger in our faith than we would have been and stronger in our love for one another."

Catriona sat back, her eyes thoughtful. "That's some story, Phoebe. I can hear your kids trying to sort it all out."

Phoebe started to laugh. "You know your cousin's story. Let's just say that every one of that group of eight, except for Adam and Noah, have gone through stuff like that. Assaults. Attempted murder. Kidnappings. Threats." She laughed again as the look on Catriona's face.   "Yes, all of them.   So, you're not alone. And Jonah's wife? Her cousin, Emma, had married Abe, and they were separated for ten years before they found one another again.   And all their friends have gone through stuff. Abe runs a security team.   Didn't stop it from happening to his men."

Catriona sat back, then reached for her cup of tea, now cold. She sipped, not even tasting it, as she thought through what had happened.

"It's hard, Phoebe.   Adam doesn't know what happened.   I don't want him hurt."

"Physically, he'll be fine.   He'll heal. It's his heart that won't, Catriona.   I've gotten to know him over the last while. He's a very private person, doesn't talk about things even with his best friends. They had no idea about you two."

"And now they blame me, don't they?"   She shoved back her chair to rise, stopping as Phoebe laid a hand on her arm, shaking her head.

"No, they don't.   They're worried about both of you. We don't know why he was attacked like he was, but they do wonder where you've been all these years. Adam has a piece of him missing, Catriona, and that piece is you. Trust him with your heart again, and trust Andrew and his team to keep both of you safe and to solve what's going on. I'm not saying it's going to be a cake walk but you do need to sit down and talk with Adam at some point again. You need to clear the air. I don't think either one of you want to move on from the other."

Catriona sat, struggling with her emotions and trying not to let the tears flow. "You don't understand, Phoebe. Carey was brutal. He was very graphic in what he said he'd do to Adam. Adam's friends? He included them as well. Now that they're married and some have little ones, how can I do this?"

Phoebe's eyes rose to Andrew who stood in the kitchen doorway. He had appeared part way through the conversation, but had stopped to listen before moving into the room. He sighed. Catriona was making this much more difficult than she needed to.

Andrew headed for the coffee pot, then sat, his cup in his hands, and waited. Catriona finally looked up, a bit startled to see him sitting there.

"Andrew?"

"He's sleeping again, Catriona, but very restless. Hannah has asked for you to come. Apparently you're the only one who can get him to settle down."

She began shaking her head even as his hand raised. "I can't."

"You can't or you won't? I think it's that you won't.   I heard what you said. Adam roused enough to hear a conversation I was having with his parents and named your brother as the one who separated you." Andrew paused to sip at his coffee. "The way I see it is that you have two choices. You can run, like you've been doing, and continue to do that for the rest of your life, messing up two lives while you're at it." He shook his head as she went to speak. "Let me finish.   Or you can go see Adam, straighten this out, let us catch your brother, and then you and Adam can go on with the life you planned. It's your choice." His eyes raised to Phoebe as they shared a look and she nodded.

"I don't know what to do, Andrew. I'm so confused."

"Then, let's take time right now to pray it through. Have you done that?" His eyes, now filled with compassion, watched as she finally shook her head. "Didn't think you had." He reached for his wife's hand and then Catriona's, bowing his head, and raising up a petition to God, asking for wisdom and strength and healing. Lord, he thought, there is so much healing here that needs to be done. Promises that were splintered and trampled on that need to be put back together as only You can do.

Catriona finally rose and headed for the door, Andrew behind her after a few quick words with Phoebe. Catriona now knew she needed to see Adam, to help him understand what she had done.

Chapter 6

Andrew shoved his phone back into his pocket as he walked towards where Catriona waited near the entrance to the hospital. He was frustrated. His team hadn't gotten anywhere with evidence taken from the fire scene. Bill had called to let him know that the fire marshal had released the scene and his team was going in. They didn't expect to find much. He'd have Adam's truck towed to their garage, to go over it, but he didn't expect to find much there either.

Andrew sent up a quick prayer as he motioned to Catriona to enter the hospital. He could tell how hesitant she was, it showed in every move she made. He gave a half smile. If he knew Adam only half as well as he thought he did, Catriona wouldn't be leaving town. He searched the area as they moved towards the elevators. He could feel someone there, but no one stood out. He nodded to the townspeople he recognized but there were a number of strangers there and he couldn't be sure that one of them wan't the culprit he was after.

Catriona paused at the closed door, drew a deep breath, then pushed it open, her movements jerky. She stepped inside, Andrew waiting in the doorway, his hand on the door. Jonathan and Hannah had gone home, he knew. Jonathan had to head into work on an afternoon shift at the plant he worked at and Hannah had needed a break.

Catriona's feet led her forward in a reluctant manner, her eyes searching Adam's face as he moved restlessly, his hands plucking at the blanket, his head turning. She sighed, knowing how hard this was going to be. You must be laughing, Lord, at this. This has to be a joke right? There's no way You'd bring me back into Adam's life, not after what I did. No, I guess it's not after all. I'm not sure what You want me to do. I just can't do this anymore.

She moved to walk away when Adam's eyes fluttered open. She froze, not wanting him to see her. Adam searched the room, his gaze stopping on her. He reached for her hand, then dropped his hand back on the bed when she didn't move forward.

"Catriona? You're here? Why?" His voice could barely be heard.

"I was asked to come. It seems people think I'm the only one who can calm you down." She moved closer, her hands gripping the bedrail.

"No, that's not true. What day is it?"

"It's a Wednesday, Adam."

He nodded. "Okay, then how long have I been here?"

"I'm not sure now, Adam. I lost track of days."

He squinted at her, the pain making it difficult to see. "You'll stay, won't you? I'm just so tired." His eyes slid closed, but his movements didn't stop.

She watched for a moment, sighed, and finally reached for his hand. At her touch, his movements stilled. His eyes opened for a moment, then closed as he slept. The nurse had entered the room, saying a few words to Andrew on the way by, and then did her assessment. She frowned and turned to Catriona.

"Are you his girlfriend? Because if you are, you need to stay. He's sleeping normally now, and his vital signs are improving." She made the notes in his chart and walked away.

Catriona stared after her before her eyes rose to Andrew. Andrew walked towards her, pulling a chair up for her.

"Sit, Catriona. Now, do you see what we meant?"

She nodded. "But I can't stay here all the time. I have clients I need to deal with."

"We realize that. Once he's good and sound asleep, we'll get you out of here. But one thing I need to make clear. You'll have someone with you all the time. You can't be out and about on your own. Do you hear me?" At her nod, he continued. "We're working through what happened at the build site, but it's slow going. Now we need to work through what you've told us about your brother. Neither one of you are safe until we get this sorted out."

She nodded, knowing her freedom to move around on her own had just walked out the door, and she didn't like it, not one bit. She really didn't want to be there, close to Adam again. She just knew she'd bring danger to him. Carey hadn't been seen in years but she knew he was still around. She'd catch a glimpse of some man that looked like him, her home would be searched, her car unlocked when she knew she had locked it. How would she ever be safe when he was still out there? She had no idea what he was mixed up in but she'd always wondered if her parents' car accident, the one that left her mom in a wheelchair and her dad dead, had had something to do with him. She'd heard voices talking when she was locked up, heard words and sentences and names she knew she shouldn't have. She had transcribed it all down and hidden it away.

"Andrew. I have some information I can give you about my brother. I have no idea what all he's mixed up in. I have it hidden away, but I can't get to it right now."

Andrew nodded, his eyes thoughtful as he watched her face. "If it helps us, then we need it sooner than later." He turned his gaze to Adam. "Does it involve Adam?"

She nodded. "It does. I just don't know how though. I can remember Carey talking about a man he worked for, and I don't think his business was legitimate." She stopped, hands to her mouth as a thought crossed her mind. "Could Carey have been involved in what happened to that home build? Has he been watching Adam and knew I was here in town and that I would be working on that build as well?"

Andrew's mind raced. Was this the link they had been looking for? "I don't know, Catriona, but we'll look into it. I need all the information on your brother you can give me. Listen, I have to run, but one of my detectives is waiting outside the door. Lily Waters. She'll talk you through this."

She nodded, then spoke, her eyes on Adam. "If I'm the cause of this, Andrew, how do I face him?"

Andrew paused, knowing what she was asking. "Talk to Phoebe, Catriona, or any of the other ladies in her group. They'll walk you through this. And most importantly, God will. He's never ever left your side."

She stared at him for a moment, as with a nod, he turned and walked away, pausing for a moment to speak with a younger woman heading her way. The younger woman entered the room and stood, her face impassive, her eyes on Catriona and then Adam.

Lily watched and waited, finally approaching Catriona.

"Do you want to leave? He'll likely sleep for quite a while longer. We'll bring you back tonight." She turned to stare at the door before looking back at Catriona. "What do you say? Wanna blow this joint for a while?" She grinned at the shocked look on Catriona's face.

Catriona sputtered, then nodded. "Please, I need to get out of here. I don't do hospitals too well. I spent too much time in one when my Mom had her accident."

"Is that right? You'll need to tell me about that, then." Lily walked with Catriona towards the elevators, then pointed to the stairs. "We only have to go down one flight. Let's take them."

Catriona hesitated, her fear of stairways rearing its head. "Please, Lily. Not the stairs."

Lily stopped, assessing Catriona before she nodded. "Sure, we can take the elevator. Not a problem." She made a mental note to talk to Bill or Andrew and run that by them.

Lily watched as Catriona paced through her workroom, gathering the material she'd need for the next day's appointment. Lily knew Catriona's mind was't on what she was doing but was in a hospital room a few miles away.

"Catriona, are you hungry? I am. I'm calling in an order to the local diner. What sounds good to you?"

Catriona stopped walked, spinning to stare at Lily. She had forgotten she wasn't alone. She finally shrugged.

"I have no idea, Lily. I don't have much of an appetite."

"That's okay.   Ev'll come up with something for you."

"I don't get it, Lily. Why are people doing this for me? I'm not from here."

"No, you're not but it's what we do." She turned as she spoke. "Listen, we need to get you home. It's getting late and it sounds as if you have a big day tomorrow."

"I do. I just hate having to do this, putting everyone at risk."

Chapter 7

$\mathscr{A}$ month later, Adam stood at the build site, his eyes on the house rapidly rising once more. The sheathing was on the walls and had the house wrap on them. He turned as he heard footsteps approaching him. The contractor stopped beside him, standing to face the building.

"How are you, Adam?" Tom Smythe, the contractor, cared deeply about the men and the trades that worked for him.

"I'm getting there, Tom. I've been cleared to work." Feeling eyes on him, Adam slowly turned, not seeing anyone but knowing someone was out there. The fear he experienced that day rose within him and he had to work to tamp it back down inside him.

"Feel someone watching you too, do you?" At Adam's startled look, Tom nodded. "I've felt that since we started the build again. I've hired security personnel to be all the time, even at night. There's something about this land someone doesn't want us to find."

"I sort of got that impression. But who? Who owned the land before you bought it?"

"A numbered company did. I have my lawyer looking into and I'm sure Andrew is as well." He shot Adam a look. "Did your memory come back? I know from your father that you had lost a few years."

"It's starting to. I can remember most of the years, but there's still some time that's in shadow."

"What about the lady you were engaged to? I hear she's our interior designer."

"Yes, she is. We're talking, dating, seeing where it goes." Adam didn't admit to anyone, even himself, that he prayed it would work out, but that for now, it was a sham, a pretence to catch the ones after them both. Adam was sure that the assault and fire were directed at him, not the contractor.

"I hope it works out. I've talked to her, seen her at church. She's a special lady.

But then she's got herself a special guy. Now, about the build. The insulation will be done this week and then the drywallers and plasters will be moving in, the painters right after them. Likely about three weeks or so before you can start. I have an idea I'd like to run by you. Can you meet me at my office later today?"

Adam shot him a look. "Okay. I guess I can. Can you give a hint?"

Tom laughed. "Always suspicious, aren't you? Can't say as I blame you. Yeah, I'll give a hint. I like your work, Adam. You're careful and thorough, don't rush it. I've been asked to take on building homes that mimic the early homes of the town, and I think your work would fit right in. You'd need to work closely with my trades, but you do that anyway. We'd been looking at probably a dozen homes or so. While you're waiting to get started here, I'll pay for you to research and travel if needed to determine just what you need to do to have the proper finishing woodwork in these homes. Drop by around 4 today." With that, Tom walked away, leaving Adam staring after him, finally remembering to close his mouth. This was a dream opportunity for him.

Adam finally made a move, walking towards his truck, apprehension rising in him as he remembered the last time he had been here. Today he was safe but for how long? Andrew wasn't any further ahead in tracking his assailants or in finding Catriona's brother. Adam needed to talk to her, to see if she would work with him on this new venture Tom had brought up. He really wasn't sure if she would.

Catriona looked up from her desk as she heard a knock at her door. She frowned, looking at the time. Mid-afternoon, and she had no clients booked. She had planned to take this as a down day from work but hadn't quite got there. She rose, determined to send whoever it was on their way in short order. She peeked through the door window and froze. Why was Adam here? Their agreement was that they always met somewhere in public, never at one another's homes.

"Adam?" The question hung between them as she opened the door.

He turned, taking in the beauty of the lady in front of him and he couldn't resist peeking at her hands. His ring was there but he didn't know for how long.

"Catriona? Can we talk? I know this isn't what we agreed on, but I had an offer today that I'd like to talk to you about."

She shrugged and then pointed back through the house. "Back deck, then. I can use a break. You'll want coffee, I suppose?"

He spun, staring at her. "Yes, please. Coffee sounds good. Can I help?"

She shook her head. "No, I already have a pot on the go. It's been one of those days."

He took the cup from her hand and then waited for her to go out first. He studied her yard. "This is nice. Very relaxing and refreshing." He took in the gardens spread out over the yard, with walkways and arches scattered among them.

"It was like this when I bought it. It was the selling point for me." She set her cup on the table and studied him. "You wanted to talk?"

He sipped his coffee, more to gather his thoughts than because he was thirsty. "The contractor, Tom Smythe, mentioned that he's planning on building a number of historical-inspired houses and asked me to do the trim work. I thought of you and how you always wanted to do something like that. Can we work together on this?"

She frowned, not quite sure what he was asking. "You mean, you and me? Together?" At his nod, she sighed and then shrugged. "I suppose. Do you have details yet?"

He shook his head. "Not yet. I'm meeting Tom at 4." He glanced at his watch. "In about ninety minutes. I'm sure he'll want you to work this as well. I'll ask for you."

"You don't have to. He'll likely call for bids."

"I doubt it. He's pretty sure what he wants." He hesitated to ask his next question. "Have you heard from your brother?"

"Carey?" She snorted. "Of course not. Unless…." Her voice died away as she rose, motioning him to follow. "I got the strangest call today. I saved the voice mail. It sounded like Carey, but I'm not sure. I didn't know the number it came from."

"Did you pass this on to Andrew or Lily?" When she shook her head, he sighed. "Catriona, you need to do this. We need to know who it is that's after you, and someone is."

"I don't know why though. The only thing Carey wanted was to break us up and that was because he was jealous of you. You were succeeding, graduating from college. You had career plans. He had nothing. He never finished high school, got in with the wrong crowd."

"I could never understand that. You two weren't raised that way. And I certainly didn't plan of keeping you away from them."

"I know, but his mind warped somehow. Mom and I can't figure it out, either."

He reached for her hand. "Come on. Lock up. We're going to find Andrew or Lily. They need this."

She shook her head. "You have your meeting."

"You can come with me. In fact, I think that's a great idea. Please?"

She stared at him, sighed and went for her purse. "Oh, all right. I don't like this, you know?"

"Yeah, you've made that obvious. But it's obvious that someone is after you too." He shut the truck door behind her and then stood, his eyes on the car waiting down the street. He could make out a man sitting there and squinted, trying to read the license plate but he wasn't sure he had it right.

"All set?" He smothered a grin at the look on her face. No, she definitely didn't want to be there.

Andrew watched Catriona's face as he listened to the message before setting down her phone on his desk. "Is that your brother?"

She shrugged. "It sounds somewhat like him, but I haven't talked to him in years. So to be honest, I can't say for sure. The wording is his, though."

Andrew nodded. "Let me have someone copy this and then you two can be on your way."

Adam glanced at Andrew and shook his head, silent communication as to her willingness to work with them passing between the two men.

"Here you go, Catriona. There's been nothing else odd that you can think of?"

She shook her head. "Just this. Oh and a sense that I'm being followed or watched."

Andrew nodded, then frowned at Adam.

"Adam?"

"There was a car with a man in it down from her house when we left. This is a description of it and what I think is the license plate but I'm not one hundred per cent sure it's accurate."

Andrew sighed. He had had enough of this, what with his friends facing adventures as they called them. "I'll see what I can find out. Stay safe, you two. I don't want to visit either one of you in the hospital again."

Adam reached for Catriona's hand, grasping it tight when she tried to pull it away from him. "Don't, Catriona. It seems strange that we don't hold hands if we're engaged. Keep up the pretence, please."

She stared at him for a moment, then relaxed her hand. She really didn't want to do this. Lord, I just can't do this. But what do I do? I love the town, the people, the work, but I'm not sure I can stay. I admit it. I'm still in love with Adam, but it doesn't seem right, what we're doing.

Adam tucked her into his truck, then looked at his watch. "Listen, I don't have time to run you back to your place. Tom won't mind you sitting in on the meeting. In fact, I know he'd welcome it."

She started to shake her head, then stopped, her eyes on the building in front of them. She was sure she had just seen her brother. Dear Lord, please protect me. I can't go through what I did all those years ago. He'll kill Adam and then me, I just know it.

"Catriona?" Adam shot her a look as he backed out and then headed towards Tom's business. "Are you all right?"

"No, I'm not. Carey's in town."

"What?" Adam almost slammed on his brakes, then pulled over instead. "What do you mean?"

"I just saw him, I think. He's changed his appearance but I would know him anywhere."

"Let me call Andrew."

Her hand reached out to his, the emerald stone in her ring sparkling in the sunshine. "No, don't. He won't be where I saw him. He'll be long gone and in hiding."

"Are you sure?"

She nodded. "Drive. You need to get to your meeting, and you're cutting it close."

The man in the car behind them cursed loudly, causing his companion to stare at him.

"What's your problem? We're only supposed to find them and watch them, reporting back to the boss."

"That's the problem. I don't want to do that. I have my own issues with those two. And I think she saw me."

"If you hadn't been so obvious, she wouldn't have. What's so important about her, anyway?"

That earned him another curse as the car headed after the two, passing the parking lot Adam had pulled into and then circling back to watch.

Two hours later, Tom sat back and studied the couple in front of him. Please, Lord, keep these two together. They are two halves of a whole. They need each other.

"We've made good progress. Good idea, bringing Catriona with you. It saves me having to persuade her to take on the interior work for me."

Catriona looked up from her notes, a blush on her face. "Thank you, Tom. This is going to be a fun project to work on."

"I think it will. And that comment just earned you two a dinner on me." He reached into his desk drawer and pulled out a gift card. "Here, Adam. Take your lady out for a meal on me. You'll be working hard in the next few months. Enjoy."

Catriona watched from the truck seat as Adam spoke a few final words to Tom, before laughing and heading her way.

"Where would you like to eat?" Adam's question caught her off-guard.

"Eat? Oh, that. You don't have to, Adam."

"But I really want to. Now, we can go eat just as we're dressed or we can go get dressed up."

"I think..... I don't know, Adam. I don't know if this is such a good idea." She stared out the window, wondering why he would want to go to dinner with her.

"It is, Catriona. Part of this is to let us be seen together, to draw out whoever is behind the attacks. You know that. And then, too, I would really like to take you out to dinner."

She turned to him, searching his face, seeing the sincerity there. "Ok, then. But where?"

"How about the little Italian place? We don't have to be dressed up to go there."

"But he gave you a gift card. Where is it for?"

Adam shook his head. "It's for any restaurant in town. That's what we do here."

She stared at him for a moment, not quite sure if that was true or how safe her heart really was any more where Adam was concerned.

The man watching them slid into a seat in the booth behind them. He was frustrated. His orders had been clear. Stop the build at that site. Find these two and bring them to the boss, dead or alive, the boss really didn't care which it was.

Chapter 8

*L*ooking up from her garden a few days later, Catriona lifted her face to the sun, enjoying the warmth. It was going to be a hot day, she thought, as she rose and headed for the house, washing her hands and the stopping in her office to pick up the folder for the new client. She paused, her eyes on the folder Tom had given her yesterday, with some paperwork she needed to go over and sign. She was excited about the new homes, just not sure if working with Adam would be the best thing for them. She sighed, knowing she needed to talk with Andrew again and was putting that off as well.

Heading out of town, she watched with interest the different types of homes, always a habit with her. She pulled up the long winding driveway and stopped. This can't be right, she thought. This building is falling down. She turned and headed back down the driveway to the highway, then pulled over on the shoulder of the road, reaching for her documents. That had been the right address, she thought, but it certainly wasn't the house the client had shown her pictures of. She pulled away, heading for Andrew or Lily. They'd want to know. She didn't see the car tailing her, dropping back as she made it to the edge of town.

Andrew looked up as the desk officer stopped at his door.

"John?"

"Catriona's here to see you or Lily. Lily's off today. Catriona says she has some concerns about a property she was to look at."

Andrew rose and nodded. "Thanks, John. I'll see her." He walked slowly to the front of the building, his eyes on Catriona.

"Catriona? Come on back." Andrew pointed to the chair in front of his desk before he sat. "What's this that John says?"

She sighed. "It may be nothing, but I can't take a chance. I set up a meeting to day to go over an interior with a client. When I got there, the building was pretty much destroyed. Dilapidated, I think, is the word I would use."

"What's the address?"

She handed over the folder. "This is the address and the client's name and phone number. Now that I've seen the building, I think it was a set-up of some kind."

Andrew skimmed through the paperwork. "You drove in and back out?" At her nod, he continued. "Good. This property has been sitting empty for ten years or more. It's held up in probate, waiting for the youngest grandchild to turn 18. And it doesn't belong to the people named here." He turned for a moment to study something behind him, then turned. "That phone number looks familiar."

Reaching for his phone, he dialled, sighing as he got the message the number was no longer in service. "It's what I thought. It's the old Grant number and it's been disconnected for a year or so now."

"Then how?"

"It's what we call spoofing, Catriona. Someone fakes a call coming in from a local number so you'll pick it up."

She stared at him for a moment, not quite following what he was saying to her. "In other words, there was no client." When he shook his head, she sighed. "How do I screen them, Andrew? How do I know who is legitimate or not?"

"That's a tough question. Just don't go out like you did today, not on your own. Find someone to go with you, preferably male."

"I can't tie someone up like that every time I go out, Andrew. People have lives they're living."

"I know they do, but I also know that they want you to stay safe, not just for your sake, but for Adam's as well." He handed over a list of names. "These are off-duty officers who will work with you. Adam's friends have volunteered as well. They're on that list. If you have to meet a new client, take one of them with you."

She stared at him, shaking her head. "I can't do that, Andrew."

"Then, what will it take? Do I need to put you into protective custody somewhere?"

She continued to stare at him. "You wouldn't!"

"Try me. If it comes to that, then I will. Someone is out to get you, Catriona, and will use whatever means it takes to do just that. Adam is at risk as well, and you need to think about that." He held up his hands as she went to protest. "Don't give me the backtalk that you don't care for Adam any more. I see it when you look at him, when you don't think anyone else is watching you. What did your brother do to you?"

She rose, anger simmered below the surface, as she struggled to contain both the anger and the fear. "I've told you. He threatened me. He threatened Adam and his family. He threatened my friends." She snatched up a piece of paper and a pen, quickly writing down some names. "Check out these people. Some will be missing. Some will be dead. The others will be too terrified to talk to you." She paused, her eyes shimmering with tears, as she bit her lip. "He's brutal, Andrew, but he presents himself in such a way that no one would ever suspect him." Slapping the paper on Andrew's desk, she turned and strode away.

Andrew stood and watched her, then shook his head. *You have yourself a live wire there, Adam.* Then his heart lifted in prayer for his two friends.

Adam looked around from where he was studying blueprints as he heard steps behind him. He frowned, not knowing who it was that approached him. He couldn't make out the face as the man had a hoodie pulled far enough forward that it shaded his face. He turned as he heard footsteps approaching from the other direction. His heart sank. *I'm outnumbered here, Lord. Now what?*

"Adam, we just want to talk with you." The first man's voice as low, but Adam frowned. It sounded familiar, but he couldn't place it.

"About what?"

The two men exchanged a look, then looked past him. Adam turned to follow their line of sight and saw a third man standing in the doorway, light behind him, his face in shadows. Adam frowned again, his mind racing. *I know that man, he* thought. No, it couldn't be. He shook his head, standing staring at him as the men behind him shared a look.

The first man spoke again. "Adam, we need your help. We represent a group in town who are concerned about the corruption in the building industry. You're involved in this area because of your line of work. We would ask you to help us find these people and then have them arrested."

"And just how do I go about doing that?"

"The house that burnt? That was done deliberately to prevent Tom Smythe from building more. The group is aware of what he plans to do and how that will bring more people and dollars to our town. This group is against that. They want to keep the tourists out and stifle the growth and economy of the town. One way is through keeping the building down."

"The home builders' association?"

"No. They're not really part of it although we suspect there is a member on the board who is involved."

Adam nodded, his eyes still on the man in the doorway before he turned back. The two men had walked away and he frowned, before turning back to the door. He stared at the empty doorway, then shook his head. There is no way that had been who he thought it was.

He stood for the longest time, eyes on the blueprints but not seeing what was there, his thoughts chasing themselves through his mind. Who was it they suspected, he wondered?

He turned once more to stare at the doorway, his thoughts puzzled before he shook his head again. He had been seeing things, he thought.

He looked up as he heard footsteps approaching him later that day as he worked in the kitchen, installing the trim. Andrew appeared, nodding as he looked around.

"This is going to be a nice home when it's finished, Adam. I like how they've kept it simple."

"It is nice. Keeping it simple means it gets done faster. And it will be easier for them to take care of with the kids." He set down the piece of window trim and studied his friend. Something was up. "You're here for a reason, Andrew."

Andrew nodded. "Catriona came to see me this morning. She went out to interview a client, but it was the old abandoned Jeffries' house."

"What?" Adam's hand went to the top of his head. "Is she okay?"

"She is. She was smart enough to turn right around and drive right back out and come see me. The phone number they gave her was a disconnected one."

"Then, how did they get that?" Adam waved his hands. "Never mind. I really don't want to know. Now what?"

"Now what is that I've told her when she goes out like that she takes someone with her or I'll be putting her into protective custody."

Adam snorted. "I'm sure that went over well." He stopped at the loud banging coming from the back of the house. "What on earth? There shouldn't be anyone here but us two. There aren't any deliveries scheduled until tomorrow."

Weapon in hand, Andrew headed out the door, his eyes searching for the source of the noise. Seeing nothing at the back, he headed for the side of the house. His head turned, he didn't see the pipe heading for his chest until he was hit and flying backwards to land, not moving, his weapon falling beside him. His assailant moved quietly towards the front of the house, his eyes watchful. Andrew was not the one he wanted. The one he was to take out was still in the house. Creeping up the stairs to the wraparound porch, he hesitated, his eyes watchful above the bandanna over his lower face.

Adam watched from the shadows just inside the door, knowing it was him the man had come for. He just wasn't sure if there was more than one. He waited as the man crept forward on silent feet until he had just passed where he was standing. A quick movement on Adam's part left the man on the floor, Adam's knee in his back.

"Who are you, and what do you want?"

The man struggled, then stopped when Adam grabbed an arm and shoved it up behind his back, finally pulling him to his feet and shoving him towards the back of the house, searching for Andrew.

Adam hesitated a moment to grab some rope that had held a bundle of trim together and wrapped it around the man's wrists before he shoved him out the door, knotting it off roughly. His eyes searched for Andrew, finally seeing him on the ground, motionless.

"You had better not have hurt my friend too much, buddy." Adam's voice was grim with worry and fear. Who was it that was after him, anyway?

He shoved the man to the ground, telling him to sit still and not move, then knelt at Andrew's side, reaching for a pulse. His head hung down in relief for a moment, before he reached for his phone and called for help.

Bill Buckley, detective on the force, watched as the patrol officers took the man into their custody, then turned to watch as Andrew shook his head at the paramedics, refusing to be transferred.

"Andrew?" Bill spoke quietly as Andrew watched towards him, hand rubbing his chest. "What happened?"

"Adam and I were talking. I came out to check the noise we heard and walked right into that pipe there."

"You're okay?"

He nodded. "Just a bruise. Could have been a lot worse. Had the wind knocked out of me, though. How's Adam?" Andrew's eyes searched for his friend.

"He's fine. He caught the guy, actually."

"He did? I wondered about that." Andrew looked around. "There was only the one?"

"There was, Andrew. They seemed to think one was enough." Adam stopped beside his friends, his eyes watchful. "You know, I don't have time for this. I'm on a time crunch here with this house. I need to have it finished in two weeks and this just set me back a good portion of the afternoon. That and the visit this morning." Adam's voice held leashed anger.

Andrew and Bill shared a glance before Bill asked. "What visit, Adam?"

"Three men. Don't ask me for names or descriptions. They made sure I couldn't identify them. They're from town, concerned about corruption in the building portion. They think I can help." He paused, a frown on his face. "I was sure I knew the third man, the one who stood in the doorway, but I can't see him being involved in something like this." He shook his head. "I think this is all getting to me."

"That's interesting, Adam. You're the seventh one I know of that's been approached like this." Andrew gazed into the distance, trying to work it out.

"The seventh?" Adam turned to stare at him. "What do you mean?"

"The six of your friends, Adam, and now you." He turned to Adam. "And just who did you think was the third man?"

Adam shook his head. "I'm not sure, Andrew, but …." His voice died away as his phone rang. He pulled it out and read the text, his face paling as he did so.

"Adam?" Bill had to repeat his name before Adam looked. "What is it?"

Adam handed over his phone, his heart and thoughts racing as he thought through the picture just texted to him.

"Adam? What's this?"

Adam looked up, fear and something else in his eyes. "That's Catriona and I from our first year of college. Who did this?"

"Her brother or one of his friends, I suspect. Let me send this on to the lab and see if they can trace it back." Bill handed him back his phone. "Now, you understand this means they're tracking both of you. I would suspect someone's done that all these years, waiting for you two to reconnect."

Adam shook his head. "How could they be? I had no idea where she was, not until I woke up in the hospital and saw her there."

"You don't remember holding her hand on the way to the hospital?" Bill had a glint of mischief in his eyes as he held back a grin.

"I did what? No way!" Adam shook his head.

"Sorry, pal. You did. You just refused to let go on her and she couldn't get her hand back. Andrew here had to pry your hand open."

Adam spun to look at Andrew, who grinned and nodded. "Well, I don't know what to say to that."

"Just admit that you've never gotten over her. Now, the task is to keep both of you safe." Andrew walked towards the patrol officer motioning him over.

"He's worried, you know. He doesn't want another friend to face what he did." Bill's voice was quiet.

"I know. I don't want to face it either, but it looks as if we may be. I just pray that God gives us the strength we need. I know this is far from over."

Bill nodded. "Now about those men today? Give me what you can of their description."

Adam stared at the house, his thoughts whirling. He described them as best as he could, then voiced his thought as to who the third man was.

Bill stopped writing, staring at him. "There's no way, Adam. Not him."

Adam nodded. "I think it was, but I can't be sure. Don't say anything, not even to Andrew. The way he was standing, he wanted his identity to be kept secret."

Bill squinted as he stared up at the late afternoon sky. "He would. He's always been big on helping his town. I'll see what I can find out, just between you and me. Look, it's late. We'll be here for a while yet. Leave me the keys and you take off. You're not going to be able to do any work for now."

Adam fished the keys from his pocket and dropped them into Bill's outstretched hand. "Thanks, my friend. Listen, it's Friday. Any plans for the weekend?"

"Not really. I'll be working late tonight. Why?"

"I was thinking of having you all over for a meal, but I'm not sure now if it's a good idea to have us all together."

Bill nodded, then spoke. "You can't stop living your life, Adam, but I get where you're coming from. I know you don't want to put anyone in danger. Let me know if you change your mind."

"I will. I have to track Catriona down. Andrew said she came in to see him today."

"She did? Interesting."

"What do you mean?"

Bill shrugged. "It's just that she's been pretty independent and not willing to admit she needs help."

Chapter 10

Standing on the back of the river, Catriona shaded her eyes against the setting sun and studied the opposite bank. Someone was there, she knew, not seeing them, just a sense of being watched. She was getting tired of this, she decided, and knew she had to do something. What that something was, she hadn't quite decided.

She heard footsteps crunching across the gravel as someone approached her and stopped beside her.

"Catriona. Should you be here like this, on your own?"

She glanced sideways at Adam. "Not likely, but I'm not hiding any more, Adam. You can if you want." She reached to pull the ring from her finger but his hand stopped her.

"No, not that, Catriona." Adam clasped her fingers. "I talked to Andrew earlier today. He stopped by where I was working."

She snorted. "Now, why didn't I think he'd do just that? He seems to think we're a couple."

"For all intents and purposes, we are, Catriona. At least until this is over. And after as well. I don't want to lose you again." She turned to him as he spoke, but he was watching the river flow by, bubbling around the rocks he could see along the shoreline. "My love for you has never disappeared."

She nodded. "Well, there's that too, isn't there?" She pulled her hand free and began to walk towards the path that would take them to the river.

Adam followed, not quite sure what was up with her. "Catriona?"

She waved her hands in the air, shaking her head at the same time. "Don't say a word, Adam. Please! This is difficult enough without you adding to it."

He sighed, digging his hands into his jean pockets. "Catriona, at some point, we do have to discuss whatever is going on between us."

"Not now, Adam. Maybe someday. But right now, it's enough that we're trying to stay ahead of whoever it is and that isn't easy when we don't know who they are." She swung around to face him.

He reached out a hand to steady her as she stumbled sideways in the sand. "I know that, Catriona, and I'm not pushing you to any decision. We need to get through this first." Adam stopped speaking, his eyes searching the area. "Catriona, come on. We need to get out of here." He turned to walk up the path but stopped as he saw the man standing there.

He spun and saw the man approaching from upriver. He grabbed her hand and, pulling her with him, began to run for the boat docks. He knew a friend had a boat there and where to find the key.

"Adam?"

"If we can get to the docks, I can get us a boat and we can head downriver for a ways. We can call for help at that point." He slid to a stop as he saw a figure approaching from the docks. "This isn't good."

"Adam?"

Adam breathed a sigh of relief. "Zeke? What are you doing here?" It was his friend, Zeke Williams.

Zeke shrugged, as his eyes traced past them to the men following. "I just had to come here. I don't usually."

"Thank you. We need to get out of here."

"Sure. Come on. My vehicle's this way. Then you can tell me what's going on." Zeke shot a glance at the two men who had stopped short of the docks. "Friends of yours?"

Adam shook his head as he drew Catriona to his side away from them. "No. I don't know who they are, but I didn't like the feeling I was getting about them."

Zeke nodded. "Okay. So you two stand right here, back to them okay. I need to take your picture. Don't forget to smile." He had pulled out a camera from his jacket pocket.

"A camera?" Catriona was shocked.

Adam started to laugh as he swung an arm around her and tucked her tight to his side. "Zeke's a meteorologist. He's never without a camera, just in case."

Catriona stared up at him, not quite sure if he was serious or not. Zeke stared at them for a moment, seeing what their friends had told him about the two. He nodded, then lifted the camera, focusing on the two men standing in the background. Hopefully, Andrew could have his team enlarge the picture and put names to them.

Zeke lowered the camera, catching the look on the couple's faces. He frowned, then nodded. He had never met Catriona before, but knowing Adam, it didn't surprise him that Adam still wanted Catriona as part of his life.

"Come on, you two. Let's get you out of here and back to your vehicles." Zeke pointed to his vehicle.

Catriona shook off whatever it was she had been feeling as she looked at Adam. No, she couldn't still love him, could she? Carey had taken care of that, she was sure.

He had beaten her feelings down where Adam was concerned, and suddenly, she wondered why she had let her brother have that much control over her. Lord, I'm not sure anymore what's going on here, but I think You do. At least I hope You do. I don't want anyone hurt because of me, and to do that I have to disappear again, just like I've been doing. And I don't want to do that. I like this town, the people, the church. Please, dear Lord, keep us safe.

Adam stood at her door thirty minutes later. Zeke had dropped them off at the parking lot and then Adam had followed her home. Zeke had promised to forward the pictures he had taken to him. Catriona stared past Adam for a moment, then studied his face. She saw the lines that had become part of it over the past few years and regretted that she had likely caused some of them.

"Adam?" Catriona's soft voice held a question.

Adam stared down at her, not quite sure what she was asking. He reached to trace his fingers on her face before cupping her cheek. He sighed, knowing he couldn't live without her, but right now it seemed as if that's exactly what he had to do. If he got any closer, he was sure somehow she'd disappear again.

"Catriona. What am I to do?" She heard the anguish in his voice. "I want you to stay safe."

She nodded, a frown marring her face for a moment, before she reached out and hugged him. He stood for a moment, then drew her close, promising with all that he had to keep her safe.

"It's like that, is it, love?" He felt her nod against his chest. "Where do we go from here?"

She sighed. "I don't know, Adam. Somehow we have to find Carey and stop this nonsense. If we don't, he'll hurt you. He promised to do just that."

"Tomorrow's Saturday, Catriona. What do you say we pack up for the day and disappear? We can go check out some of those historical homes Tom wants us to."

She stilled, then nodded. "Okay, I guess. I just wish I felt safer."

"Do you want to take anyone with us?"

She leaned back. "I'm sorry?"

"We can take some friends with us. Maybe we'd be safer in a group rather than on our own."

"But that would be putting others at risk."

"I know, love, but it's up to you. I can make some calls and find a couple to go with us. Maybe Josiah and Faith?"

She shook her head. "Not Josiah. Carey would go after him as well if he's there." She stared past his shoulder, studying the darkening sky and the stars just starting their twinkling, tracing over to stare at the new moon peeking out of the midnight blue sky. "No, maybe just us."

"Okay. Now, go on in and lock up after yourself. I'll see you in the morning."

Catriona stared up at the crown moulding and other trim in the historical house they had stopped at on Saturday morning before turning to Adam. She laughed as she saw the camera in his hand.

"Taking notes, are we?"

He looked over at her, then down at his camera before joining her in laughing. "I guess I am. This place is fantastic. So many ideas to run by Tom. How about you?"

She nodded, her eyes alight with ideas. "Tom's houses can be a real showcase of what you can do with simple ideas." She looked over at Adam again. "Thank you, Adam. I needed this."

"We both did." He reached out a hand, waiting for her to take his. When she did, he interlaced their fingers, walking with her back through the house and then down the street to where he had parked. "I never knew there were so many older homes that you could visit."

She nodded. "There are many. I always found them, wherever I lived. Some people just want modern stuff, but my clientele seems to be gravitating towards what we just seen."

"You'll have to showcase your business that way. Historical interiors."

She stopped, pulling him to a halt with her. She stared into the distance as he patiently waited for her to move. When she didn't, he gave a tug on her hand. Surprised, she stared down at their hands and then up at him, a softening coming to her face and eyes. *Lord, I have no idea where I'm going here, but You do. I think I'm finally ready for this.*

"You okay?" Adam's voice held a question.

She nodded. "I finally think I am, Adam. I'm ready to move on." Adam's heart sank at her words. "Let's find some place we can talk. That talk you wanted? It's time."

Adam tilted his head to study her face, but she kept her face neutral, no matter how fast her heart was racing. *Yes, Lord, he's the one, always has been. Now, You just need to protect us and get us through whatever it is that Carey has decided to put us through.*

"Are you sure?" At her nod, he helped her into his truck, shutting the door after her, praying that he wasn't shutting the door to his heart and having to let her go. As he slid behind the wheel, he looked around, feeling the eyes on him, but not seeing anyone who stood out. "Where do you want to go?"

"How close are we to our college town?"

"Oak City? About ten miles. Why?"

"Can we go to that park we liked? Pick up some sandwiches or something and eat there." She looked over at him, a look in her eyes that he couldn't read even as he nodded.

Two hours later, Adam crumpled up the papers from their lunch and walked over to deposit the trash into the can, standing for a moment with his back to Catriona, trying to gather his thoughts and emotions. He had no idea which way this would go. Please, Lord, keep us safe. I can feel that evil around us. He turned and walked back towards her, meeting her halfway there. She reached for his hand and tugged him along the path they had walked many times before.

She walked in silence for a few moments before she spoke. "I was so afraid, all those years ago, Adam, that Carey would kill you. You don't want to know how he described it to me. I have to live with that. I don't want you to. He also threatened your parents and your friends. I couldn't let him hurt you, and he had friends that would have vouched for him, making it out that I was the one giving the threats." She drew a deep breath, feeling the emotions rising within her once more and not liking them.

She stopped, her eyes on Adam's face, as he watched her, a question on his face. "It has been so hard, Adam, to live like I have, knowing that if I were to contact you in any way, Carey's threats would come true. I never thought about it being your hometown. I just wanted a small town to live in and to grow my business. I don't want to put you at risk."

"What I've gone through may have nothing to do with Carey, you know. I wish you had talked to me, other than just that note. But wait, that wasn't you, was it?"

She shook her head. "It was Carey. He forged that note and tried to pull the ring from my finger one night when I was asleep. I woke up as he was doing that and tried to stop him. I found it where he had thrown it across the room in anger." Tears welled in her eyes and she willed them back down. "I have a scar from where he hit me. My hair covers it now."

Adam drew a sharp breath before enveloping her in his arms. "I wish I had known. I'm sorry, Catriona. I never knew."

She nodded, her hair brushing against his chin. "I know. But I'm done running and hiding from him." She leaned back so she could look up at him. "If you'll still have me, Adam, my answer once again is yes. I have never stopped loving you. Fear drove it deep. I can't live in fear any more. But I'm not quite sure how or where we go on from here."

Adam studied her face, seeing the resolve there to end it all. "We'll figure it out. Right now, put Carey out of your thoughts. We need to just enjoy today for ourselves."

Catriona nodded as she stepped back out of Adam's arms, her eyes searching the area around her. "He's here, Adam. Somewhere, out there, he's watching us."

"I know. We'll take precautions, keep our eyes open. Now, what would you like to do? I have enough pictures I think to work with for now." He searched her face. "I know exactly what I want to do."

She stared at him. "Adam?"

He pulled her at a run back to his truck, laughing as he tucked her inside and then ran around to slide behind the wheel. "I need to get you something special, love."

"Adam!"

An hour later, she stared at the heart-shaped locket as he fastened it around her neck. "Just something, love, to seal our commitment." She turned to look up at him and he reached to hug her, a kiss dropping on her lips.

"Now what, Adam?" She sighed. "I think that's become our theme song."

He started to laugh as he led her from the jewelry store. "It just may be, you know." He stopped for a moment. "I guess we have to head home, don't we?"

She nodded. "Eventually, we do." She sighed. "I don't want to. I want to leave everything behind and find some deserted island where no harm could come near me."

He laughed again, knowing he felt the same way, drawing her close.

Phoebe nodded to the couple the next morning as they left church, drawing Andrew's attention to them.

"They seem different, Andrew. What changed?"

He stared after them. "I'm not sure, Phoebe, but something did. Did you invite them over for lunch like we talked about?"

"I did, but Adam said they had plans. I'm not sure, but I think they've come to some sort of agreement."

He shrugged. "They may have. Listen, let me take you out for lunch then."

Adam watched Catriona as they walked up the path to his parents' home. "Are you sure?"

She nodded. "We need to tell them, Adam. We need to warn them to be very careful."

He agreed. He had not had a lot to do with her brother but had never liked him. His instincts had been right about him. Now, how did he protect his lady love and his parents?

Hannah and Jonathan stared at the two sitting at the table with them after they had explained everything, before exchanging glances.

"Catriona! We never knew! How could he be like this? He's not like your Mom or you." Hannah rose to go and hug the younger woman.

"No, he's not. Nor like Dad. Mom and I could never figure it out, other than he became part of a gang."

"You never told us that when you talked about him." Jonathan shared a look with Adam, a frown in place.

"I never knew for sure until after I got away from him. He had his friends looking for me. They threatened Mom if I didn't come back home."

"They never did, did they?" Adam's voice was tight as he asked.

"No. For some reason, they backed off. Mom always maintains it was the angels surrounding her that scared them away."

"What all was he involved in?" Jonathan spoke, his eyes on Catriona.

"What wasn't he involved in? I can't begin to name what all he was suspected of. That's why he went into hiding. Just after I got away, the police were looking for him to question him about a murder."

"Murder? That changes everything then." Hannah turned to Adam. "And just how are you going to keep our girl safe?"

"Our girl?" Adam started to laugh. "Mom!"

"Well, she is." Hannah watched as Catriona and Adam looked at each other. "Okay, you two. You're up to something. Spill."

Adam laughed even harder as his father joined in. "Your language, Mom. You're talking like one of the kids you teach at Sunday School."

She smirked. "We teach one another. So, what's going on?"

Adam reached for Catriona's hand. "We had a long talk yesterday. Both of us still care deeply for one another and have decided we're not going to let Carey win. We're starting to make wedding plans, but we're working through what we've been through first."

"That's a wise move, Adam, Catriona. Take your time. You need to get to know one another again. You've grown, changed, and right now, you're likely facing a huge barrier." Jonathan reached for his wife's hand and then Catriona's. "Let's pray, you two, and ask for protection for you during the next few weeks."

Chapter 11

*A*dam threw down the hammer he was holding and ran for the door of the house he was working in. He had received a call from Catriona and, just after he answered, heard a woman scream. He couldn't tell if it was her or not, but he was taking no chances. The dial tone worried him. He quickly called Andrew, letting him know what was up and heard Andrew's quickly indrawn breath.

"Did you know Catriona was meeting with some of the ladies today?" Andrew's breath came rapidly as he too ran for his car, calling out for patrol officers to head for Catriona's home.

"No, I didn't. Oh, no! How many?"

"All our wives, I think Phoebe said." Andrew's voice died away for a moment, and Andrew could hear him talking to someone else. "I just asked Bill to start calling the fellows. They'll meet us at Catriona's."

Adam stood with his friends, his eyes glued to the door of Catriona's house as he watched Andrew, Bill, and the patrol officers enter. A few minutes later, they returned.

"Josiah?" Andrew walked towards him. "Weren't the ladies meeting Catriona today? And here?"

Josiah nodded, a grim look on his face. "They were. They're not in there?"

"No, they're not. Call Faith. I don't want all of you calling your ladies at the same time. We'll stagger it until we can get one to answer."

Josiah nodded even as he dialled his wife's phone. "Going to voice mail, Andrew."

Andrew nodded. "About what I expected. At five minute intervals, the rest of you call your wives. Adam, come with me for a moment." Andrew waited, turning back when Adam didn't respond. "Adam?"

Adam lifted his head, then handed his phone to Andrew. "Catriona just got off a text to me. The women were separated.

She's with Aideen. She's not sure where the rest of the women are."

Samuel's face paled. "Are they okay?"

Adam nodded. "Catriona says they are. She's trying to find an address or landmark for us." He looked around at his friends. "I'm sorry, my friends. I never expected this."

The men shared a look, then Jonah spoke. "Adam, we understand. We've been through this and you know it. Who would have thought someone would have taken all our ladies." He looked down at his phone. "Andrew, Candace just sent a text. She and the rest of the ladies are out at the old mill. They were dropped off there."

Andrew spun and then turned back to the patrol officer standing near him. "Call for back up and get out there. I'll need to stay here." He was torn, wanting to go find his wife, but needing to stay where he was.

Bill approached. "Go with them, Andrew. Lily's here and can run this. I'll take the fellows back to the department."

Andrew nodded before searching the faces of each of his friends, his eyes lingering on Samuel, who he knew was worried about Aideen, and then on Adam, knowing Adam was worried the most.

"Adam?" Andrew waited until he looked up. "God is with us, my friend. Don't lose sight of that. Let me know if Catriona comes up with a landmark."

Adam gave a short brisk nod before he turned and walked to his truck, shoulders slumped. This was his fault, he thought. His fault and now his friends' wives were put in danger.

Matthias watched him walk away before he spoke. "He's blaming himself. He shouldn't. Who would have thought that our wives would be in danger when they were together?"

"I'd like to get my hands on her brother." Josiah's anger at his cousin simmered just below the surface. "I knew Carey had a mean sadistic streak, but not to this extent. I can't imagine what he put Catriona through when he held her captive."

At his words, the men stopped walking and stared at him.

"Held her captive?" Mark Benson laid his hand on Josiah's arm. "What are you talking about?"

Josiah drew a deep breath. "Remember how quiet Adam's been for the last few years, not dating or anything?" At the collective nod, he continued. "He and Catriona dated all the time they were at college. They were planning their wedding when Carey kidnapped Catriona and held her captive for six months. He forged a letter from her telling Adam she didn't love him any more and that the wedding was off. He also threatened my aunt, Adam, his parents, and our close friends."

"You've kept this really quiet, Josiah." Mark turned to look back at the house, as he hit the button on the key fob to unlock his doors. "I can see why, but who did this? Was it your cousin?"

"We don't know for sure. Catriona says she's seen him here in the area, but she not one hundred percent sure that it's him. Andrew's been working on the case."

Adam watched his friends head for the vehicles and pull away. His prayers were with their ladies, before his thoughts turned to Catriona. Where would Carey take her? He pulled out his phone, searching for another message and not seeing one. His eyes stared at her home, and then he was out of the vehicle, heading for the shed at the back, ignoring the calls of the officers.

He cracked open the door to the shed and hesitated. He stepped inside and looked around. Surely, he hadn't had this thought, that something was left inside, without God leading him. He stared around at the neatness of the building before his eyes lit on an envelope. He sighed and turned to go find Lily. He had been right.

Lily carefully lifted the envelope, her eyes on Adam. "How did you know, Adam, that something would be here?"

"This is a game to him, Lily. He's playing with us. That's why he took the ladies. That's why he left that." He pointed to the envelope, then paused as his phone chimed. "Excuse me." He pulled it out, a frown on his face. "Lily, where's the nearest abandoned quarry?"

She looked up from the letter in the envelope. "South of here, about 20 miles. Why?"

"Because that's where Catriona and Aideen are. Catriona just sent me a text stating they were dropped off there. And it's a big area to search, isn't it?"

Lily nodded, even as she sealed the letter into an evidence bag. "It is. I'll have to call in search and rescue to go in. This note now makes sense."

Adam reached for it, his eyes on Lily's face for a moment, but she gave nothing away. She stepped outside the shed to call Andrew and then the search and rescue group. She prayed that Tad and his wife would be the ones to respond. Walking to the door, she asked for some clothing of Catriona's and then called Bill for him to get the same from Samuel for Aideen. She looked up. Rain was moving in and it would be there likely before they found the two ladies.

Adam read the note, his heart sinking at the cruelty contained in it. He had no doubt that Carey was behind this and that he would do exactly as he said, kill Catriona and anyone else who got in his way. His heart lifted to God. Please Lord, not this. Keep our ladies safe. Guide us to the safe conclusion of this.

He handed the letter back to Lily and walked away, not hearing her call after him. His eyes searched the area, focusing on a man standing under a tree. He walked towards, eyes narrowing.

"Where is she?" Adam planted his feet shoulder width apart and stared at him.

The man grinned, yellowed, broken teeth evident. "He said you'd find me. Come with me and I'll take you to her."

"Really? And how do I know you'll do just that?" Adam wasn't about to step into a car with this man, but he needed to hear what he had to say.

"Then I guess you really don't care about those women, then do you?" The man turned to walk away, stopping short as he saw the uniformed officers standing behind him. "This won't work, pal. If you arrest me, you won't find her."

"You know, I think I might. The other ladies have been found and are safe. My lady and her friend? I know where they are and am heading that way."

The man shot him a mean angry look. "You won't win, you know? He's got an enormous group of people to help him."

"If you're talking about Carey, not really. Once he has no access to his money and can't buy his friends, they'll desert him. If it's Gray, then he won't win either."

The man stopped, his mouth opening and closing, his eyes narrowing in hatred. "You think you have it all figured out? You don't."

"Maybe. Maybe not. But I do know that whoever is behind this won't win." Adam walked away towards his truck, missing the speculative glance Lily shot him. She would need to talk to Andrew and see what he had to say.

Weapon drawn, Andrew pointed towards the broken door hanging by one hinge. The officers with him nodded and then spread out around the abandoned mill. He wasn't sure if they would find the ladies there but he could see evidence of multiple footprints, a number of which were female. He pulled the door back, cringing at the loud grating and squeal he heard. He squinted as he stepped inside, waiting for his eyes to adjust to the dimness. He searched where he could see before he moved forward, pointing to his officers to search the building.

Reaching a door with a new hasp and lock on it, he paused, breathing a prayer. He pointed to the door and the officer with him nodded. Holding up three fingers, Andrew counted down, then the two men kicked at the door. It took a few kicks but the weakened door finally fell into the room.

Andrew's weapon was raised as he entered, his eyes searching the room, before they lowered to the women sitting on the floor, hands clasped, fear on the face. Then Phoebe was on her feet and in her husband's arms.

"Andrew. I knew you'd come. Where're Catriona and Aideen?"

Andrew holstered his weapon and tightened his arms around his wife. "I'm so glad you're safe. Let's get you all out of here and then I can get a team in here." He looked up at the other ladies. "Everyone's okay? They didn't hurt you?"

"No, they didn't. It's so strange, Andrew. They just wanted Catriona. I don't know why they took Aideen too." Faith spoke as she stopped beside him before walking out of the room.

"Let's get you back to the department and to your men. We'll talk about it then. I'll need statements from each of you." He turned to the officer with him. "Have Bill bring out the passenger van from the church or have Silas do that. We need to keep these ladies together for the trip back."

The officer nodded and headed for the patrol vehicle, his eyes searching the area, not seeing anything that would alert him.

The man stood under the trees, watching as the women filed out and were then seated in the van. His rifle was trained on Faith, following her progress, before being turned to Andrew. He had his orders, but now wasn't the time to take the shots. He would have too much difficulty getting away.

Adam stood on the edge of the quarry, his eyes searching for anything that would help him find Catriona and Aideen. Where are they, Lord? The quarry had been abandoned long enough that trees and underbrush had grown up covering the bottom of the hole. He knew there was a lake or pond in there somewhere as well.

He turned as he heard footsteps approaching him, and he frowned. He didn't know this man.

"You're Adam?" The man stopped short, his eyes watchful, a kind look on his face.

"I am. Who are you?"

"I'm Peter Gregg. I heard that you are looking for your lady and a friend."

"How'd you hear that?" Adam's brows drew down as he stared at the man.

The man laughed. "I'm sorry. I didn't introduce myself properly. I'm part of the search and rescue team for the county. Tad asked me to come by and see if you were here. Lily seemed to think you were." He pulled out his wallet and handed his identification to Adam.

Adam relaxed a bit. "Tad? I thought he'd be here."

"He's away on a training course this week, and his wife is with him. Listen, I have my dog down at the entrance in my truck. How be we head down there? The growth is too thick to see much from up here."

Adam nodded. "I know. I've walked around the edge and don't see where anyone was forced over the edge."

"I don't like that thinking." Peter shook his head. "But I can see how you'd think that." As they walked back down to the entrance, Peter shot a look at Adam before he spoke once more. "We've got more teams coming in, but so's the rain. How be you and I team up and start searching?"

Adam nodded as he reached to unlock his truck and then retrieve a sweatshirt Catriona had left in the back. "Here. Will this do?"

Peter nodded. "It will. I was hoping you'd have something of hers with you." He headed for his truck, reaching to release the door on the truck cap and then opening the crate door to let out a beautiful red and white Border collie. "Amy, girl, we've got work to do." He reached to fasten on a different collar and the dog's demeanour changed from play to work.

Adam stood and watched, finally walking after Peter and his dog, hoping they'd find the two women before the light mist that was falling became a full-blown rain. He shrugged his slicker collar up higher and pulled his ball cap down further.

"Peter?" The man turned as Adam caught up to him. "How's this weather going to affect the search?"

"It will. We'll do what we can with Amy before it rains too hard. If you're a praying man, pray hard."

"I have been." Adam frowned as he saw Amy acting differently. "What's up with her?"

"She's alerting. See. She sat. She found something." Peter motioned Adam to stay back as he walked towards Amy. "What'd you find, girl?"

Peter searched the area, finally pulling back some branches and then froze.

"Well, hello! Who do we have here?" He turned and motioned Adam forward.

Heart beating fast in anticipation, Adam stood behind Peter. "Aideen? Thank God! You're fine." He reached out a hand and pulled her to her feet. "You are okay, aren't you?"

She nodded. He could see the tear tracks on her face and the fear in her eyes. He wrapped an arm around her and walked her away from her hiding place.

He watched Peter as he placed a call to Andrew before he turned to Aideen.

"Where's Catriona?"

She shook her head. "Somewhere in here, I think. We were together until a bit ago. Then, they separated us." She shuddered, fear crossing her face. "I went through so much, Adam, but nothing like this. I don't know where your lady is or what they plan."

He nodded. "We'll find her. First we get you back to Samuel." He turned as he heard footsteps behind them.

Andrew paused for a moment before approaching Aideen. "You're okay? They didn't hurt you?"

"I'm fine. Samuel?"

"He's fine. He's waiting back at the entrance for you. I'll send you out in a moment. Can you tell us anything."

She shrugged, pacing in the small space she was allowed. "Nothing. They never said a word. I never got a look at their faces." She frowned. "But Catriona seemed to know them. No, not her brother, if that's what you're thinking. Maybe friends of his?"

"Friends? Okay. I'll let you get back to the department." He nodded to a patrol officer to head out with Aideen before turning to Peter, the rain starting to fall heavier. "Where do we stand now, Peter?"

"We can track for a while, but if the rain gets heavier, we'll need to stop." Peter turned to his dog, calling her to continue her search.

Amy cast around for a few minutes, then headed towards the back of the quarry, her tail wagging slightly as she followed the scent trial.

Peter turned. "Well, are you coming or not? Amy won't wait."

Andrew shook his head as a small smile crept across his face. His eyes studied Adam, seeing the devastation and fear there, and remembering only too well how he had felt with Phoebe.

"Ready to move, Adam?"

Adam looked up, then after Peter, before nodding and moving after the search team. He could heard steps behind him and knew Andrew and his officers were there.

Amy led them deeper into the brush, her nose moving constantly as she sought to find Catriona's scent. Adam studied the path they were following and finally turned to Andrew.

"How many do you think, Andrew?"

Andrew shrugged. "It's hard to tell, with the rain. I would say three and Catriona." He stopped for a moment, looking around. "I don't see anyone walking back out but they could have gone out a different way." He didn't say anything more but he was deeply concerned. If they had taken Catriona in too far, his team might not reach her before the rain became too heavy and washed away the trail and the scent.

Catriona buried her head in her knees, her arms clasped as best she could around her knees. She had fought the men who had brought her here, fought hard despite her hands being bound. She had rubbed her wrists raw trying to loosen the bonds but hadn't succeeded. She finally raised her head, her hair in bedraggled stands on her wet, muddy face. She had fallen a few times, yanked back to her feet and pushed further forward. She had no idea where she was. She shivered as the temperature dropped and the rain became heavier. She looked around, not seeing the man who had stayed behind to guard her.

She clumsily climbed to her feet, her eyes searching the dimness. She moved quietly, away from the area she had last seen the man and hoping she was moving towards the entrance of the quarry. Her head tipped back for a moment as she studied the walls and then she sighed. Even with her hands free, she'd never be able to climb the walls.

She stopped, hearing a noise from behind her, and moved behind some brush, crouching down to hide herself. Her guard walked by, his eyes searching for her. She sighed. Now, he was in front of her. Which way did she go? She rose, heading back the way she had come, finding a small animal path to follow that she prayed would lead her out.

Peter finally called Amy to heel, turning to Andrew. "I have to call her off. The rain's too heavy right now for her to work. I'm sorry." His eyes were on Adam as he spoke.

"We understand. What are the chances of Amy picking up a scent trail in the morning?"

Peter shrugged. "Not sure, Andrew. Depends on how well preserved the trail is. Right now, she's struggling. I would suggest we regroup in the morning and send in teams. I can stay around here overnight

with Amy and if the rain stops, go back in."
He stopped as he heard rustling and
breaking branches.

Andrew turned, motioning to his team,
and pulled out his weapon. The man who
staggered into sight froze and turned to run,
stopping as the officers ordered him to his
knees. He finally raised his hands, dropping
to his knees, and locking his hands behind
his head. His head hung low. He had failed.
The man who had hired him had told him
that if he failed, he was a dead man, no
matter if he was in jail or out.

Andrew turned in a circle, searching
for Catriona, before approaching the man.

"Where is she?"

"Where's who?" The man squinted at
Andrew through the rain running down his
face. "I'm here by myself."

"No, I don't think you are. You were
left to watch the woman you kidnapped. We
know that for a fact. It will go better for you
if you talk."

The man glared at Andrew. "I want a
lawyer."

Andrew's hands rose in the air at that. "Brown, take him back and book him for eight counts of kidnapping, one of assault. We'll sort out the rest of the charges later." He watched the officers walk away with the man, then turned to find Adam. "Now, where'd he go?"

"Who, Adam? He was right here." Peter turned in a circle, then watched Amy. "Where'd he go, girl? Did he walk off that way?"

Amy gave a low woof, her tail swishing back and forth, as she looked up at her master.

"He didn't, did he?" Andrew groaned, looking down at his watch. "It's after 10. Surely he's not planning on walking around here in the dark. I don't remember him having a flashlight."

"He didn't and I would hazard a guess that he's following the trail our friend here left. I'll head after him. I have supplies in my pack."

Andrew nodded. "I'm going to leave some officers here at the entrance if you need them. Here's the number you can reach them at. Take care of him. He's not thinking straight."

Peter shook his head. "No, he's thinking hard and straight. He knows his lady is in here, and he's determined to find her. Leave them with me. I'll get them back for you." Peter whistled for Amy and walked off, leaving Andrew staring after him.

Now what did he just mean, he thought? No, Adam's not thinking with his head. At least, I don't think he is. Please, Lord, protect them. Bring them out of this safe. And guide me now as I have to work through this with the ladies, including my own. Andrew turned to walk back towards the entrance, stopping as he heard a sound.

He spun, trying to determine exactly where the noise had come from. He walked backwards on the trail, stopping as he saw the brush moving, his hand going to his weapon.

"Catriona?" He walked rapidly towards her as she stumbled from the brush and fell. He knelt, rolling her over, and then reaching for his pocket knife to release her bonds. "Catriona, can you hear me?" She didn't respond, her eyes sliding closed.

He reached for his radio, sending in a call for help, then for his phone.

"Peter, are you with Adam?"

"I can see him just ahead. Why?"

"I have Catriona. She just made it out herself. Catch him and bring him back."

Adam stopped and turned as he heard his name yelled out from behind him. A frown crossed his face. Why was Peter here and why was he stopping him?

"Adam. We need to head back." Peter absentmindedly rubbed Amy's head and ears.

"Why? I need to find Catriona."

"Andrew has her. She made her way out. Come on. Let's get back out of here."

Adam stared at him. "She's out? She's okay?"

"I have no idea, but we need to head out of here. Andrew was taking her out to the paramedics he called for. You'll likely need to meet him at the hospital."

Adam brushed by Peter and Amy, his hand landing for a moment on the dog's head before he tugged his ball cap down tighter and headed back the way he had come. Reaching the entrance to the quarry, he looked around, not seeing Andrew or Catriona. One of the officers approached him.

"Adam, Andrew went with Catriona. If you'll let me have the keys to your truck, Andrew asked an officer to bring it to your place, and for me to bring you to the hospital."

Adam stared at him for a moment, then nodded, his hand finding his keys in his pocket and handing them to the officer. "How is she?"

"I can't say. All I know is that I'm to take you to the hospital." He looked past Adam at Peter, who nodded and headed for his own truck, lifting Amy up to her crate and reaching for a towel to dry her off.

Adam slumped in the seat, his eyes not seeing the rain cascading off the car windows, his thoughts on Catriona. Please, Lord, let her be okay. I don't think I can handle it otherwise.

Andrew looked up as he heard the door to the Emergency Department swish open and saw Adam enter, the patrol officer right behind him. Phoebe raised her head from where she had been resting it on Andrew's shoulder and watched.

"He looks rough, Andrew."

"He will be. They'll not let him in for a bit." He watched as Adam ran his hands through his hair, shaking the wetness off before he came and slumped down into a chair.

He finally raised his eyes, to stare at Andrew and Phoebe.

"Phoebe, you're okay?" At her nod, he turned to Andrew. "The others?"

"They're all fine and home with their guys. Samuel just took Aideen home."

"I'm sorry, Andrew, Phoebe. This shouldn't have happened." He stared at the floor, not hearing if they responded, before he shifted in his seat to stare at the doors to the examination rooms. "How is she, Andrew?"

"She's alive. I don't think she was mistreated. But the rain and the stress took their toll, Adam.   The physicians are working with her now. They told me about another thirty minutes and someone could go in."

Adam nodded.   "Thanks, Andrew." His head went back on the wall and his eyes closed. Andrew and Phoebe shared a look, not sure if he had fallen asleep or was praying.

Chapter 12

Catriona glared at Adam as he stood in front of her, hands on his hips, preventing her from leaving her hospital room. She spun around, thumping her bag back onto the bed.

"Catriona?"

"Go away, Adam." She stood, her back stiff, not looking at him.

He sighed, then approached her, hands going to her shoulders. "Don't shut me out, love. We need to work together on this."

She shook her head. "Knowing me is putting everyone in danger. I can't go on like this."

He turned her to face him, finally putting a finger under her chin and raising it. "Look at me, love." He waited. "Catriona, look at me."

She looked at him, shaking her head. "I've put everyone at risk."

"No, you haven't." Adam searched for the words, desperate to make her understand before she walked away from him. He knew that if she did, he would lose her forever.

"But I have. If I hadn't been with the ladies yesterday, they would have been safe."

"Actually, Catriona, that's not true." The two spun to see Bill standing here.

"What do you mean? Of course it is."

Bill shook his head. "No, I've talked with the man we had in custody. He had nothing to do with your cousin. So it wasn't because of you. We're still trying to figure out the motive, but we'll get it."

"What?" Adam swung an arm around Catriona, anchoring her to his side. "Then who?"

"That's what were working through, but it seems to be related to all the incidents that have gone on over the last few years."

Adam groaned. "So it was me?"

Bill shook his head again. "Not necessarily. Why? You did get a visit from a group like the others."

Adam stared at him. "The others?" He frowned. "There were three. The man who didn't talk? I felt like I knew who he was, but it couldn't be him." He pursed his lips as he thought, then frowned again. "No, it couldn't be him. He's not even in town."

"Who were you thinking of? The same one you mentioned?" Bill watched with interest the conflicting emotions crossing Adam's face.

"No, I won't say, because I'm not sure it was him. Whoever it was seemed to want to keep his identity a secret."

Bill frowned. "So, you're not saying, then. Well, I guess that's that." He turned to look behind him at the door. "We need to get you two somewhere you'll be safe."

Catriona stomped towards him, anger in her manner. "I'm not hiding away anywhere, Bill. Get that through your head. If Adam isn't going to take me home, I'll find a ride myself." She returned to the bed, grabbed her bag and was gone before either one of the men could react.

Adam shook his head and then ran after her, catching her as she entered the elevator, sliding in beside her just as the door closed.

"Go away, Adam." She stood arms crossed, her bag over her shoulder.

He reached and pulled her close to him. "Not happening, love. We're in this together. We'll get it figured out."

"Before who gets killed?" She stared at the door, willing it to open, not willing though to let him know how much she needed him.

He reached for her hand as the doors swished open and led her to his truck. "In you go. Now, who do you have to meet with today?"

She stared ahead, not answering for a moment. "I have a meeting with Tom."

"Okay, so do I. Let's combine the two and then see what happens afterwards. Where are your drawings?"

"At home." She stared at him for a moment, anger flickering just below the surface. "I don't want you hurt, Adam. No one else either."

He shook his head as he parked in her driveway and reached to stop her from getting out. "Let me get your door."

He held out his hand and waited while she stared at it, before she lifted her eyes to him. She finally reached for it and he pulled her towards him, enveloping her in a hug before turning her towards her home.

"Let's get your paperwork and then go find Tom." He stopped at her door. "Did you lock this behind you?"

She looked around him. "I did." Then she sighed and pulled out her phone. "We're not going in, are we?"

He shook his head and moved her over to sit in the swing on her front porch. "Sit here. It'll be a while. I'll call Tom and let him know what's happening."

"But Adam, what about the house you're working on? Shouldn't you be there?"

He shook his head. "I'm waiting on some trim to come in. It's a special order and won't be in for a couple of days. So, no problem." He pulled her over tight to him. "What about you? What clients are you needing to see over the next couple of days?"

She chewed on her bottom lip as she watched the officer walk up from the street. "I have three I'm taking in new designs for. And I have to go to Oak City to source some material for two more." She laid her head down. "I just can't do this anymore, Adam."

"I know, love." He looked up at the officer. "Ted, thanks for coming. It looks as if someone has been inside Catriona's home over the last couple of days."

Ted nodded. "Let me take a look, and then I'll come back. Any animals I need to watch for?"

She shook her head. "Maybe that's what I need to get. An attack cat."

Ted stared at her as Adam spluttered, trying to contain his laughter. "An attack cat, huh?"

She nodded. "Yep. They can be very sneaky. You don't see them until they're on top of you."

Ted shook his head as he walked away, a small grin twitching on his face.

Ted returned shortly and stood in front of them. "I don't see anything disturbed, but I can see mud throughout. Before you go through, I'm going to have a team take samples and fingerprints. Then, I'll walk you through to see what you find."

Adam pushed his foot to get the swing moving, his thoughts on Catriona, and then changing to prayer.

Andrew stood for a moment, watching them. He had heard the call come through and sighed as he did. What next, he wondered?

"Andrew?" Adam's voice broke through his thoughts.

"Can't let you two out of my sight, now can I? Catriona, how are you feeling?"

She shrugged. "No side effects from yesterday, at least not that I know of. I didn't need to come home to this, though."

"No, you didn't. When you're through here, I need to bring you two up to speed on what we've found out. It can wait until you're done."

Andrew finally sat down in the rocking chair of the porch, his eyes on the street. He frowned as he studied the car sitting there, before reaching for his phone and calling for a patrol car to come back. He didn't have a good feeling about that car.

"You wanted to talk to us, Andrew?" Catriona's soft voice caught his attention.

"I did. Are you sure you both are up for this?" At their nod, he continued, "The man who separated you and Aideen yesterday is not working for your brother. He's not saying who he's working for, though, and he doesn't have an arrest record. The name he gave is false. He did say that the men who abducted all you ladies are from out of town. We're still working on the whys of that."

"It doesn't make sense, Andrew. Why take all of us? Which one of us were they really after?" Catriona shared a look with Adam.

Andrew nodded, seeing how Catriona had gotten right to the heart of the matter. "That's what we don't understand. We don't know if it's related to your brother or to the matter Adam has been asked to be involved in."

"Adam?" Catriona stared at him. "What matter?"

"A group came and asked me to help bring down whoever it is that's involved in the criminal activity with the home builders here in town."

"And you're just telling me now?"

"Catriona, it just happened. We haven't had a chance to talk yet, not with what happened to you."

"What about Carey?"

Andrew shook his head. "Haven't seen him, but I have had word he's in town. Have you seen him at all?"

She shrugged. "He's likely changed his appearance since I last saw him. I've seen someone who reminds me of him, but I couldn't say for sure that was him." She looked at Adam. "So, we're no further ahead in your investigation, I take it?"

"We're ruling out people, but we still have stuff to work through.   Don't do anything foolish, Catriona." His glance was stern, as she stared back, a blank look on her face. "I've seen some of the other ladies try stuff."

"And what would I be trying, Andrew?" She stood. "I need to go through my house, and then Adam and I have a meeting."

Andrew stood, his eyes on her, then on Adam. Adam followed her into the house and watched as she went from room to room. She finally turned to the two men. "There are some photos missing. Ones of Adam and I from college. One of Mom and I from a month or so ago."

"Anything else?"   Andrew made a note of what Catriona had found.

"No, not offhand.   Was it Carey or someone working for him?"

"We found some prints, so we'll see if they match anyone." Andrew pocketed his notepad. "I'll be in touch. Stay safe, you two."

Adam watched as Catriona talked with Tom a while later. He could see the stress in her face. He shook his head, then concentrated on what the two were talking about. A chime from his phone had him excusing himself.

"Adam? Andrew."

"It must be important if you're interrupting me in a meeting, Andrew. What did you find?"

"Her brother was in her place as well as two friends of his. The three of them have long records. I don't like this."

"You and me both. So now what?" Adam turned to watch Catriona.

"Will she go somewhere safe, do you think?"

Adam snorted, causing Andrew to laugh. "Not likely. I can try and see if she will."

"That's what I thought you'd say. Then, we need to come up with a plan." He paused, and Adam could hear him rustling papers. "The man we picked up yesterday is a known cohort of one of the men. But I can't guarantee he was working for her brother."

"No, you can't. Not unless you can prove it. I still think there's more than one party involved."

"I suspect you're right. Listen, keep her safe. Lock her up somewhere. Bill and Lily are working like crazy trying to connect all the dots for us."

"I'm sure they are. I need to go and get back to my meeting. Call me with any new developments."

Carey stood outside the office, leaning against the building, his eyes staring through the window at the three inside before he looked down at the photos he was crumbling in his hands. He was angry and desperate and broke and needed someone to pay for his state of financial destitution. His sister was the one he blamed. She would pay for what she had put him through.

Chapter 13

Catriona looked up as Adam walked towards her, a tray of drinks and bags of food in his hands. She wasn't hungry, but she knew she needed to eat.

Adam finally sat back, his eyes on the trees behind her where they sat at a picnic table near the downtown area.

"I spoke with Andrew this morning." He waited, but she didn't say anything. "Your brother was in your home."

"That doesn't surprise me. He'd be the one who took those photos. Who else was with him?"

"A couple of his friends. Andrew didn't name them. But the man they arrested for kidnapping you was known to one of the friends."

"This just keeps getting better and better. Why, Adam? Why were we taken?"

"That no one seems to know yet." Adam eyed his drink, popping off the lid to look at the ice at the bottom of the cup. "I have no idea who or why. Andrew's working as best he can but he has other investigations that he needs to be following, not just ours."

Catriona nodded. "Then, we research what we can." She slipped from the seat and reached for his hand. "Come on, Adam. You need to get to work and so do I. Let's meet tonight to work through our ideas. And I have lots."

He swung his arm around her as they walked back to his truck, tucking her tight to his side. "I'm sure you do, love. Do we need to bring in anyone else?"

She shook her head. "For now, just us two, okay? After the ladies being kidnapped, I don't want to endanger anyone else at this point." She stared at her clasped hands. "We're missing something, Adam, and I just don't know what."

"Have you talked to your Mom lately?"

She shook her head. "No, I haven't." She sighed as she rested her head against the window, her eyes drifting closed. "I want this over with."

Adam gave silent consent to that wish, knowing that it wasn't by a long shot, and he had no idea of how long it would take.

Adam sorted through the papers that Catriona handed him, not sure what he was looking for. He stared around, then rose and headed for his truck. Catriona stood, their cups in her hand, frowning. Now where was he, she wondered, her face clearing as she saw him returning, a roll of paper in his hand.

"What's that for?" Catriona pointed with his cup before handing it to him.

"I want to lay out what we know, what we suspect, who we have involved. That kind of stuff." He looked around. "Where can I lay it out?"

"Dining room table, I think. We can extend it and I'll put some plastic underneath the paper"

He nodded, his mind already racing with what he needed to figure out. He absentmindedly accepted his cup, sipping at it, then grimacing at how hot it was. Catriona started to laugh as he glared at her.

He set his cup aside and rolled out the brown Kraft paper, reaching for a pen when he finished. He started writing, Catriona coming to stand beside him, her hands cupped around her mug before she pointed.

"Why them?" She was surprised to see he had listed various members of the construction trade.

"We know something is going on with the construction trade here in town. We need to consider each one of the men and women involved. Do you have some painter's tape or something that won't pull the paint off the wall?"

She nodded, heading for the kitchen and returning with a roll of green tape. "Here. Where do you want to hang it?"

"Where's a good spot?" He looked around, not quite sure.

Catriona set her mug down and headed to take down some pictures, setting them on the floor to lean against the wall. "We can tape the paper up here, I think. It should work. How many are we going to have any way?"

He shrugged. "I have no idea. Now, let's talk about your cousin. Who were his friends that you remember?"

She nodded. "I see where you're going now. Okay." She started giving names, almost faster than Adam could write. She finally stopped, standing back and staring at the paper, her hands rubbing at her arms.

He shot her a quick glance and then looked down at the names. There weren't many but someone on that list other than Carey made Catriona very afraid.

"Which order would you put them in?" He handed her his pen.

She chewed at her lips, her eyes thoughtful as she read the list of names, her hand finally moving to the paper, numbering them as he asked. She threw the pen down finally and stepped back. He could feel the fear emanating from her and reaching for her, drew her into a hug and then just stood, waiting for her to relax against him. Her arms finally reached around him, and he pulled her tight, his cheek coming down to rest on her hair.

"I won't let them hurt you, if I can at all prevent it." He made that promise to her, not knowing what the future would hold, but with God's help, he was determined to make it come true.

She finally nodded, then spoke, her voice muffled. "Now what, Adam? Where do we go from here? We have names. We know something about them. But we're not detectives. So how do we proceed?"

He thought for a moment. "Candace's cousin runs a company we can approach. They track people and find out things about them even the police forces can't. We can start there."

She sighed. "This is more complicated than I thought. Okay, contact whoever it is you need to. I just want this over."

"You and me, both, Catriona. I don't like what's happening to you. I want to keep you safe and I can't."

"I know. I want the same for you. I feel like someone's following us every step we take, that they're sitting outside watching our homes, our families, our friends. We've seen the steps they'll take. We have to do something to prevent this from happening again." She leaned back so she could look up at him. "How do we do this, Adam?" She stopped, a look of fear crossing her face. "My Mom. Is she safe?"

He stared down at the face of the woman he was deeply in love with. "Would she come here to visit? It wouldn't take many modifications to make your home accessible for her."

"She might. It would be getting her here. It's a four hour trip."

"Then, how about on Saturday, we go up and get her?"

Catriona finally nodded. "Let me call her and see if she'll come here for now. I'm so worried about her."

"I know you are, sweetheart." He pulled out his phone as it chimed, frowning at the text message, his heart sinking as he saw the picture, knowing someone was outside the house watching them. "First, though, let's get this to Emma at Trackers or Jace. They'll work their magic."

She moved away to grab a pad of paper and started writing names, her hand stilling. "Adam. That one. He's the one who's behind this. Not Carey. Carey doesn't have the brains or know how to plan an attack like this."

"Are you sure?" He read the name she had circle and his heart sank. "I think you're right. Listen, Samuel's father's a forensics investigator. I can get him to look into financials on this man."

"Please do. We need all the information we can gather to take to Andrew."

"Speaking of Andrew, have you heard from him today?" When she shook her head, he sighed. "I was hoping he'd have news. What about the guys' ladies?"

"I talked to Phoebe and Aideen. They're okay, just puzzled like we are." Catriona began to pace, her thoughts whirling, a memory niggling at the edge of her thoughts. "There's something, Adam, that I can't get through to my mind. I don't know what or who it is, but it's important to this."

"Pray about it, love. That usually works." He watched her as she paced. "Is it a person, event, thing?"

"That's the thing. I don't remember." She pulled at her hair. "It's frustrating." She stopped to stare at the wall where he had hung the paper with the town people's names on it. She frowned and walked over to trace a name. "Who is this?"

"Her? Stella Forsythe. Her family's been involved in the building trade in this town for probably sixty years, mostly supplying concrete or cement to the commercial sector."

"I've never met her, but I know her name. Now, why?" She spun to stare at him. "How old is she?"

He shrugged. "Around our age, I think. Her father's getting ready to retire and she's taking over. He's been sick, so she's been running the business for about seven years or so."

"Did she go to college?"

Adam nodded, his thoughts on the woman. Then, he frowned. "She did. Our college."

"Was she a partier?"

He nodded, comprehension dawning on his face. "She was. Into the bar scene and those who knew her suspected drugs as well. She hid that if she did them, and no one could ever prove it. You think she knows your brother?"

"I do. Adam, what have I brought to town?"

"It's not you. Your brother would have gone after anyone. He's going after you just because you defeated him. You're likely the only one who ever got away from him." He frowned. "Do you know if he did anything like this before?"

She shook her head. "I have no idea, Adam." She pulled back a chair from the table and sat, her hand reaching for his pen and idly doodling on the paper.

"How'd you get away from him in the first place?"

She shrugged, her eyes on her hands. "I really don't know. I was so out of it by that point. Hungry. Thirsty. Beaten down. Mentally and emotionally broken. I remember trying the door and it opening. It was always locked. I just walked out and walked home. I don't remember that but the police told me I walked ten miles that day." She looked up at him, a shuttered look in her face. "Mom was desperate to find me. It had been six months. Carey played them all, pretending to help look for me, all the while laughing to himself because he knew exactly where I was."

"I can't even imagine how your Mom felt."

She shrugged again. "She's never really talked about it. I was so sick for a while after that. I have trouble with locked rooms now, though. I don't like them."

"That's understandable." He began to compose an email to Emma, sending off the names as they had labeled them. "We should have an answer on some by tomorrow. If Emma's knows it's for us, she'll make it a priority." Then, he groaned. "What did I just do!"

Catriona stared at him. "What do you mean?"

He shook his head. "I just contacted Emma. She'll tell Abe and he'll want to bring in a security team to keep us safe."

"What are you talking about? Security team?" Catriona really had no idea what he was talking about.

He nodded. "Emma's husband, Abe, has a security team. He also has a couple of friends who have them, one right in this town."

She shook her head even as she laughed. "That's not happening. You can tell them that."

"Yeah, right. I know these guys too well." He looked around the room. "So now what? What do we really know?"

"Just some names. I wish we knew more. We need to list occupations, contacts, how they might know each other. That might work."

"We do, but it will have to wait for another day, love. It's getting late, and we both have things to do in the morning."

"Do we need to talk to Andrew?" Catriona really wasn't sure of anything any more

"I'll call him tomorrow or send him an email. Let me know the names you've remembered. He'll look into them. I'll call Samuel's dad, Barnabas, as well to search out that one man's financials." He turned to hug her, dropping a kiss on her cheek. "Lock up after me."

"I will." Catriona watched him drive off before she sighed and moved back to the dining room, her eyes searching both lists, trying to find a connection between the two. She was sure there was, but just not who.

She reached for her phone. She really needed her mother and the most she could do was talk with her on the phone. It would have to do, she decide, heading for the kitchen to make another cup of tea.

Finally heading for bed, she stopped in her office. Something was off in there, but she just wasn't sure what. She paced the room, studying everything and making sure the windows were closed and locked. She stopped, fear suddenly coursing through her. What was it that was in here? What had Carey done?

Chapter 14

$\mathcal{T}$wo o'clock in the morning found Catriona up and in her office, walking through it again. She just knew something was off. Something had been added to the room and she was determined to find whatever it was. She searched along the book shelves, sighing to herself as she pulled books off and then replaced them.

Finding nothing with the books, she frowned, her eyes turning next to the framed pictures. She searched those, then turned her attention to the few ornaments she had sitting around. She felt them carefully, trying to think like her brother.

Then, she studied the furniture, feeling over her desk chair and the two upholstered chairs. Next came her desk. She searched it thoroughly and found nothing. Heading for the kitchen to her tool box, she stopped. And turned. And saw it. The way the light reflected she saw the object hidden in the cold air vent. She froze. If there was one there, where else would there be one? She sank to the floor, her arms around her upraised legs, chin on her knee, staring at the camera, or what she thought was a camera. She shook, knowing that Carey would likely have seen what they were doing and heard that they were planning on bringing her mother to her home.

She finally rose, heading for the kitchen. Lord, when will this be over? I know I can depend on You, that you keep Your promises to us. But I am just so tired of all this. Why can't I have had a normal brother?

Dipping the apple spice teabag in the hot water, she stood, eyes staring at the doorway to the hall before she glanced at the clock. She had been searching for four hours. She sighed, dumped the teabag into the garbage and set her cup on the counter before heading for her bedroom. She reached for her phone after dressing and stared at it. She knew Adam would be up, but could she call him this early? She shoved her phone into her jeans pocket and walked back through to the kitchen, grabbing her cup and Bible and heading for her back deck. She just needed some God time this morning and the early morning light beckoned her to the back deck.

Three hours later, Bill stood in her office, watching as a tech carefully removed the object from the cold air vent. He had a team searching the house once more and they had found other similar objects in the kitchen and living room.

"What is that?" Catriona stood near Bill, her finger pointing at it.

"It's a listening device. Not a camera like you thought." He took the bag the tech handed him. "Is this the only one in this room?"

"So far, Bill, that's it for here. The team found one in the kitchen and one in the living room. None anywhere else. We'll look outside as well." The tech turned to Catriona. "Just curious. What made you search in here?"

She shrugged. "Just a feeling that something was off. I knew Carey had been in my house and this would be about his level of activity."

The tech nodded, opened his mouth to speak and then walked away after a glance from Bill.

"We still haven't found your brother, Catriona."

"I didn't think you had. Look for the criminals and drug addicts in town. He'll be with them." She shivered, her memories hitting hard.

"Are you okay?" Bill was worried about her and pulled out his phone.

"Don't call Adam. He's at work and needs to stay there. If you call him, he'll leave and come here. I don't want that." She stared Bill down.

Bill nodded. "If you're sure. You mentioned something about your Mom." He handed the evidence bag back to the tech.

"I am. Adam and I are to go up there on Saturday. Mom has agreed to come here for a bit. Now, I'm not so sure if that's a good idea."

"Let me talk to one of the detectives in her town and see what we can work out for her." He paused, a sparkle of mischief lighting up his eyes. "You know what's going to happen now, don't you?"

She turned, a frown on her face as she narrowed her eyes. "And what would that be?"

"Andrew will want to lock you up somewhere you'll be safe." He laughed at the look on her face.

"That's not happening, Bill." She spun on her heel and marched over to her desk. She reached to gather the folders she needed for that day, pausing to drop her head and say a quick prayer for guidance. "I have an appointment with a client in an hour, Bill, across town. Are your techs just about finished?"

He nodded, then realized she had her back to him. "They are, about ten minutes I think."

She turned, her eyes on him. "Good. Then I can lock up. Let me know what you find out about those."

He nodded again, then spoke. "You need to be very careful, Catriona. If your brother has placed these, then he's likely aware of what you're planning and where you will be. Make sure you're aware of what's going on around you."

She stared at him, then shook her head. "If you're done, Bill, I need to finish off this paperwork and then leave."

Feeling dismissed and not liking it, Bill turned to find the techs had left. He stood on the driveway, his eyes searching the area. Someone was out there, he knew, but he just wasn't sure where or who.

Adam turned back to the door as Catriona pulled it open and then walked out towards him. He frowned. This wasn't normal for her.

"Can we walk, Adam?" She leaned to look down at his feet. "Good, you're in sneakers."

"We can." He reached for her keys to look her door. "Around your neighbourhood or somewhere else?"

"Around here, I think. We need to talk and away from the house."

Adam reached for her hand, drawing her close to him. He waited as they walked, his heart lifted in prayer for his lady.

"You're not talking, love. Bad day?"

She shrugged. "It was a great day with the clients. I was able to find what the one couple wanted and sort out issues there. I met with a new client and have to put together a proposal for them to go over and see if it works. It's a limited budget and will be a challenge." She hesitated to continue. "I searched my office early this morning. Bill came in with his tech team and found listening devices in the cold air returns in the office, kitchen and living room."

Adam's steps hesitated for a moment, then gripping her hand tighter, he continued their walk, his mind racing at the possibilities and dangers this brought forth. "Your Mom? We talked about bringing her here."

She nodded. "I asked Bill about that. He was arranging for her to be hidden away for now, at least until this is all sorted out." She swiped at the tears on her cheeks. "I hate this, Adam. I hate living like this. He's taken far too much away from me. Too much time. Too many friends."

Adam's heart hurt for her lady, hearing her express her frustration and hurt. This shouldn't have happened, he knew. What had driven Carey to become what he had become they might never know. All Adam knew was that he wanted to wrap Catriona up in his arms and take her away from all this. Hide her away until it was all over. But if he did that, it would never be over. At some point, Catriona would have to face her brother.

He pulled out his phone as it chimed. He had been expecting a call from a fellow contractor about a problem he had run in to on the job site. Instead, he frowned. It was Emma.

"Emma? Good to hear from you. It hasn't even been twenty-four hours." Adam nodded at the question in Catriona's eye and pointed towards a bench in a small park.

"Adam. What have you gotten yourself mixed up in?" Emma's voice held worry. This was not like her, he knew.

"What are you talking about? All I asked was for you to run some names for me." Adam reached for the pad of paper and pencil he always carried in a shirt pocket.

"I know you did. Have you any idea of what's going on and who's involved?" He could hear her rustling papers. "I've sent on what I've found to Andrew. Adam, you need to be so careful. These are very dangerous people, involved in who knows what all. I talked to Abe. He wants to bring you both here and tuck you away."

"That's not happening, Emma. Neither one of us can leave our work. We have commitments that we have to keep."

"I know that, and so does Abe."

"Talk to me about these people, Emma. We need that information in order to make a proper decision on what to do."

Emma sighed. "I told Abe this is what you would say. Let Catriona know that Micah and Luke headed over to her Mom and are bringing her here to the compound for now"

"That's great news. Wait. Let me put you on speaker so Catriona can hear as well."

"Catriona, I'm Emma. We've never met but I look forward to that."

"Me, too. Now what was it you were saying to Adam to make his face go white?"

"Oh, dear. Did it?" Emma's soft laugh came over the air. "Just that who you've gotten mixed up is very dangerous."

"I know that already, Emma. He's my brother. I've been there."

"I know you have, but your brother has gotten much worse. From what I can find out, he's gotten in deeper and deeper with some people who are not so nice. I told Adam that two of Abe's men are heading for your mother's place and are bringing her back to our compound. No one will get near her here."

"Thank you, Emma. But what did you find out that we need to know about?"

They heard more paper rustling, then Emma's voice speaking quietly to someone. "Jace is heading your way now. He wants to meet with you and Andrew and Bill. But I can tell you that word has been put out on the streets that Carey wants you, Catriona, and will pay a huge amount of money to get you."

Catriona's face whitened. "That can't be right. Why?"

"First, because you got away from him. Second, he's been watching you apparently and you're back with Adam. Third, he thinks you have some information that will lead him to a huge payout."

"What? That's not possible. I have no information like that. My clients aren't rich. I'm still making a name for myself. Dad didn't leave much. Mom has only had what she's been able to earn on her own. Any settlement from the accident has gone to making her life more possible and comfortable."

"I know you don't. We all do. It's just that we've been told your brother thinks this. He'll come after you or Adam, to get to you. Right now, he and his friends have gone into hiding."

"I figured that. Bill found listening devices in my home this morning. Taking them out will set him off again, I'm sure."

"That it will. Now, Adam. That Forsythe woman you asked me to look into. She's not a very nice lady, now is she?"

Adam snorted. "Confirming what I already know? I've known her all my life and she's gone from bad to worse. Rumour here is that the family company is just one step away from bankruptcy. I have someone looking into the financials."

"Good. That's what I have for you right now. I'll be back in touch as soon as I can. Like I said, Jace will be there. He left about an hour ago. I have spoken with Andrew and Bill."

"Great!" Adam and Emma started to laugh at Catriona's reaction. "He's going to lock me away somewhere. I just know it!"

"Not necessarily, Catriona. Work him though. He just wants to keep you safe. Catch you two later." Emma was gone before they could ask anything more.

"Is she always like that?" Catriona stared at Adam, shocked with how abrupt Emma had been.

Adam laughed. "She is. Her mind runs so fast, very few people can keep up with her. Abe can. So can Jace. She thinks of things no one else does and she finds things other investigators can't find. She thinks outside the box, as they say." His arm around her, he snugged her closer to him. "But where do we go from here, Catriona? You're definitely not safe."

"Nor are you." She shrugged before laying her head down on his shoulder and yawned. "I'm sorry. I didn't sleep much last night. I was searching my office, trying to find what Carey had done."

"Listening devices? So they likely know what we were doing. I don't remember us saying names out loud, other than his and Shelley Forsythe."

"No, we didn't, but I can guarantee he'll find her." She shuddered, her mind going back to what she had suffered at her brother's hands. "I don't want to be where he can get me, Adam, but how do we avoid that? You're not safe, either. He'll use you to get to me."

Adam was only half listening to what she was saying, watching as a car slowed and stopped near the park and two men exit it. "Come on, Catriona. We need to get out of here. I don't like the looks of those two men." He rose, grabbed her hand and pulled her with him, his pace rapid.

She shot a look back after them. "They're following us, aren't they?"

"I do believe they are. This park looks like you can't go any further than the trees, but there's a hidden path that only people in the neighbourhood would know how to find."

"You're not from the neighbourhood. So how do you know about it?"

"I had a cousin who lived in this area when we were young. We used to explore here a lot. I just hope we can get along it."

Adam pushed aside some brushes and shoved Catriona onto the narrow trail, pulling the brushes back behind him. He was praying that the men hadn't seen them come in there. He held a finger to his lips, motioning for Catriona to walk ahead of him. He heard the curses and rough words of the two men and felt relief that they hadn't found them but he knew it was only a matter of time before they did. How did he keep his lady safe when he wasn't with her? He knew she would absolutely refuse to have one of the security teams he knew with her. And he couldn't really blame her. He felt the same way himself. He brought himself up short, almost running into her as she stopped at the end of the path.

"What is it?" His voice was quiet.

"Where are they, Adam? Have they followed us or come around this way?"

He searched the area. "I don't see them, but we still have to get back to your place. And they'll be waiting there for us." He slumped against a tree, his hand running through his hair. "What did I do, Catriona? I thought I was getting you out of there."

"And you did. We just need someone to pick us up and take us back to my place. That way you can get your truck and I can lock myself inside the house"

"That's not going to work. He's proven he can get into your house. You're not safe there."

She shuddered. "I know. I just don't know where to go." She willed the tears back down. Carey wasn't worth crying over, not any more. She had shed enough tears over him. She was done with being afraid of him. "We need to go on the offensive, Adam, instead of hiding and trying to keep out of their way. I need to find him."

"You can't do that, Catriona. He'll kill you. You do know that, right?" Adam's heart clenched as he thought of what Carey would do to her. "You'll disappear again and no one would ever find you. I can't do that again, not having you back in my life."

She nodded. "I am well aware of that, Adam. I don't like it any better than you do. Do you have a better plan?"

"Besides locking you away somewhere with ten foot walls and a moat?" He grinned as she elbowed him. "Other than that, no."

"But what about you? You're not safe either." She slumped against him as he drew her into his arms. "What are we to do?"

"Get married?" She frowned at him at that. "No? That wouldn't work, I know that."

"No. It would likely make it worse." She turned to look around them. "Do you think it's safe to head back to my house?"

"We can try it. Come on, then." He reached for her hand, then stepped back into the shade of the trees. "Wait. I don't like how slow that car's moving. Yes, it's the same one. Now what?"

"Now we call for help. Did you get a plate number?"

He shook his head. "No. Just a make and colour." He turned his head to look behind him before looking out at the street again. "We can't stay here all night. Let's go. We just have to trust that we make it back to your place in safety."

They walked rapidly, their heads turning as they searched for the men. They didn't see Carey walk out of the park and follow them, his phone in his hand. He had them, he thought, then paused as a patrol vehicle approached.

"Lily?" Adam bent to look into the window. "What are you going out here and in a patrol car?"

She laughed as she shrugged. "Going back to my roots, I guess. I've been looking for you two. Andrew wants to talk with you and sent me out to find you when he couldn't reach you on your phones."

"That's strange." Catriona commented as they both pulled out their phones. "I don't have a call from Andrew tonight."

"Neither do I."

"Get in. I'll take you to find Andrew." She waited until they were seated and then drove off, leaving Carey staring after her, his mind wondering what was going on.

"Andrew? You were looking for us?" Adam's voice roused Andrew from his paperwork and he nodded, pointing to the chairs in his office.

"Sit. I need to talk to you." Andrew's keen eyes watched as the two sank into the chairs. He didn't like the looks on their faces. "What have you two been up to now?"

"We went for a walk, sat and talked, and then had to run and hide." Adam's eyes were on Catriona as he spoke. "Why?"

"What are you talking about?"

Adam filled him in. "And then we found Lily, who says you want to talk to us. What about?"

"I received a message from Emma. Know anything about that?" At their nod, he threw the papers he was holding down on his desk. "Didn't we tell you not to get involved in the investigation?"

"You did. But it's my life, Andrew. I can't sit back and watch and wait for Carey to strike. He's close to me now. I can feel him everywhere I go. I can't continue to live like this." Catriona was not backing down from the anger she saw flaring in Andrew's eyes.

"You have to leave the investigation to us. We can't keep you safe if we don't know what you're doing."

"It's our lives, Andrew. If we choose to investigate and then find someone who can look into something for us, then we will. If that's all, I'm out of here." Catriona stood and walked away.

Adam stared after her, then turned to Andrew. "You had better have good reason for this, Andrew. Friend or police, you need to work with us. I won't have Catriona upset and walking away from me." He too rose and walked from the office.

Bill stood and stared after them, then looked through the door at Andrew. "That went well, I take it?"

Andrew sighed. "I never even got a chance to get to what Emma sent me." He stared down at his papers before rising. "We need to find them again, Bill. Emma's found information that suggests Carey's ready to make his move. Catriona won't live if he does."

Bill nodded as he headed for his car. "And somehow, I don't think that's going to be very easy."

"No. I suspect we'll have trouble finding them. You head for Catriona's. I'll look around the downtown area."

Andrew searched the downtown area, then moved his search further from that area. *Where are they, Lord? How could they disappear so quickly?* He pulled his phone out as it chimed.

"Bill? Any sign of them?"

"No. But they've been to Catriona's. Adam's truck is gone. It looks as if there were more than them here. The grass is disturbed, almost as if there had been a struggle of some kind."

"That's not good. I'm heading your way. Call it in. Get the license plate to patrol." Andrew was angry but he was also very worried. His conversation with Emma had been unsettling, to say the least.

Emma's call had come out of the blue to him. He hadn't expected Adam to contact her. She had forwarded the lists the couple had made and Andrew was surprised at some of the names on it. He had given it to the detectives to look into. Emma's comment that Catriona's mother would be at Abe's security compound also surprised him, but it shouldn't have. It's what Abe did. How he wished he could lock Adam and Catriona somewhere safe like that, or at least pull in Richard or Don and their security teams to take them into protective custody.

Catriona would fight him on that, he knew, but that was the next step. Either a security team or some of his officers and right now with all the investigations they had going and were just finishing up with, his small team of detectives was stretched thin and wearing out. He needed to find a way to relieve the pressure and let some of them have time off.

He sighed as he parked in front of Catriona's and watched as the team scoured the area, and then as one of the techs exited the house. He frowned at that. Catriona was too careful. Why was her home unlocked?

"Bill? The house is unlocked?"

Bill turned as Andrew spoke. "It was. Her keys are on the floor and the mats are disturbed. The team's going through there now." Then he pointed at the yard. "We found evidence that Adam was tackled there and taken down. His wallet was on the ground. It looks as if they took the two and Adam's truck as well." Bill looked around at the houses. "It seems odd that no one saw or heard anything. Whoever it was timed it right."

"They just left us, Bill. How did they get them so quick?" Andrew spun in a circle, trying to think through what happened.

"I know. They've been followed, that's what happened." He pulled out his phone, frustrated at its ringing. "It's Lily. Lily? Anything?"

"Not at Adam's. It's locked up tight, Bill. His truck's not here. I've walked the perimeter and don't see anything out of the ordinary. How about where you are?"

"They were here, Lily, and we have signs of a struggle, inside the house and on the lawn."

"I don't like that. I'll head your way, Bill. Anywhere else to look?"

"Try Adam's job site for one. Wait. Doesn't he have a cabin somewhere?"

"Not that I know of. Does he?"

Bill searched his memory. "I think he does or his parents do. Let me work on that and I'll get back to you."

Bill hung up from Jonathan. That lead didn't work. They had sold the cabin a few years ago to a friend who had renovated it to a year-round home. Now where, Lord? Where do we search?

Andrew approached both Bill and Lily as they leaned against the patrol car Lily had been driving.

"No signs of them?"

Bill shook his head. "Every lead we think we have doesn't pan out. Where did they take them?"

"I have no idea and we need to find them and fast. I just spoke with Emma. Catriona's mom is safe. I have asked Richard to go to be with Jonathan and Hannah. Barnabas called. He has some financials on Shelley Forsythe Adam asked him to look up. He's sending them to my email.

"Emma has been trying to trace Carey's steps, and it's been difficult but she's managed to track him to some motels here in town but he's not there when I send an officer there. We need to find him. If we find him, we'll find the two."

A commotion behind them caused Andrew to spin and then walk rapidly to where three officers were restraining a large man. They struggled to take him down, finally handcuffing him as he lay on the ground, protesting that he just wanted to talk to them. Andrew motioned for them to pull him off the ground.

One of the officers pulled the man's wallet and opened it, questioning him as to his identity and then reading him his rights.

Andrew accepted the wallet, his eyebrows rising at the name. He flipped the wallet closed and handed it back to the officer.

"Okay, Everett. You wanted to talk. Now talk."

The man shook, from what Andrew wasn't sure. He swallowed hard and then spoke, rapidly telling them what they wanted to know.

"Where is Carey now?"

The man shook his head. "He had two or three locations. They're in my wallet. But that's not the problem. If he doesn't get what he wants from his sister, he's prepared to sell her to the boss."

Andrew's face whitened and grew stern. "And how do you know this?"

"I was there when he agreed to do this. You need to get her away from him." The man's eyes widened and then he slumped, the officers springing to catch him, eyes on the widening red splotch on his back.

The officers all ducked, weapons out as they searched for the sniper and didn't see him.

Bill crouched beside Andrew, his eyes on the paper with the locations, calling them in. "Do you think he was legit?"

"Someone did. We need to find those two. But which place are they at? Have the officers approach with caution and call us if they spot them. In the meanwhile, keep searching for locations." Andrew paused and pulled out his phone, searching for the text message from Emma. "Here. Add this location to the search. Emma seems to think

it was important.   Maybe those two just
helped save themselves after all."

Chapter 15

 Seven days later, Andrew sank gratefully into his chair, weary to the bone, beyond exhausted. He had had little sleep, averaging three hours a night in the last few days.   Too many investigations were entering their last stages, and too many investigations were beginning.   His detectives were stretched thin, and beginning to show the stress. He was no closer to finding Adam and Catriona. Adam's business was sitting there and the home owners were concerned. Jonathan had managed to find a friend to step in and work through the plans Adam had laid out.

 Catriona's customers were concerned but content to wait, as long as it didn't go too far.   Jonathan and Hannah were in constant contact with him as was Catriona's mother. Abe had offered his men to help in the search as had Richard and Don. At the moment, Andrew didn't know where to search. Every location they had come across had been searched and searched again.

He looked down at the pile of paperwork on his desk and sighed, reaching for the phone to call his wife. He wouldn't be making it home until late, if then. A noise at his door had him on his feet and reaching for Phoebe.

"What brings you here, love?" He took the bag she was holding and set it on the desk.

"I just wanted to spend some time with you. I know you won't be home until late. I brought us our supper."

Andrew wrapped her in a hug before pulling her over to the couch where he gently shoved her down before retrieving the bag.

"This is wonderful, love. I was just about to call you." He watched her face, seeing something there. "What is it?"

She shrugged, then pointed to the covered dish in his hands. "Eat. Then we talk."

He studied her again before he peeled back the lid on the dish. "Oh! Wonderful!

Your roast beef and veggies. This will certainly hit the spot. Now tell me about your day."

They talked quietly as they ate until Andrew wiped his mouth and fingers on the paper napkin, dropping it into his dish and covering the dish with the lid again. He reached for Phoebe's dishes, placing them back into the bag, then reaching to wrap her close to him.

"Thank you, love. That meal was wonderful, but more wonderful that you're here, in my arms. But you have something on your mind."

"There is, Andrew, and I'm not sure how to explain it." She studied their linked hands. "It goes back to when we were all with Catriona that day. We were talking and one of us asked her about family. She just said she had her Mom who was disabled and a brother who she hadn't seen in a number of years. That her father was killed in an accident. Somehow, when she said that she changed." Phoebe looked up at Andrew. "Maybe it's being married to a police officer, but I don't think it was an accident, not in Catriona's mind. The look on her face said differently. It was such a brief glimpse that I got. Could her brother have been responsible?"

Andrew watched his wife's face, his own face calm, but his mind racing. That was something he knew he hadn't even considered. "That's a possibility, love, and one I'll certainly look into. What else?"

She shrugged. "It was an impression I got that the men were surprised to see all of us that day. That we were taken, not because of what happened, but as a scare tactic directed at Catriona. Aideen was sitting next to her. I think that's why she was separated from us." She paused, lost in thought. "It wasn't very well organized, that day. They seemed off, that it was rushed. I don't think her brother organized it. From the little that was said, I think it was someone he owed money to or had something that belonged to them."

"You didn't say any of this in your statement, love. How come?" Andrew's head was tilted to watch her face.

"Because it was all an impression I had, not solid." She looked at him, tears pooling her in her eyes. "Will this help get her home?"

"It might. What else do you remember?"

"I think one of them was named Everett. That name slipped out and he was mad that it did." She shook her head. "Other than that, I can't think of anything." She stood, looking down at him. "Will the name help?"

Andrew rose and hugged her once more before picking up the bag and walking her to her car, his thoughts far away. "Not him. He was killed seven days ago when we apprehended him at Catriona's. A sniper got him."

"Andrew!" Phoebe's steps stopped. "Now what do you do?"

"We keep looking. If you or any of the other ladies remember anything call me. Drive safe, love." He reached down to kiss her, then shut the door behind her, watching as her car drove out of sight before he turned to head back inside. He stopped, his face raised to the darkening sky, his thoughts chaotic as he prayed for wisdom and peace, before lowering his head and heading back for his desk. Bill stood waiting for him.

"Bill?" They turned to walk into the building and towards Andrew's office.

"I tracked down where Everett was staying. I have a team over that and they've sent me an address."

"Whereabouts?"

"Near the lake in those abandoned cabins. I'm just heading in to set up a team to go search it. Lily's working on a search warrant just in case we need it."

"Whose cabin?" Andrew sank into his desk chair.

"The old Forsythe one." Bill was looking at his notes and finally looked up at Andrew's silence. "Andrew?"

Andrew shook his head to clear it. "The Forsythe place, you say?" He searched through the papers on his desk, finally finding the one he wanted. "Adam and Catriona were doing some work on their own the other night. Shelley Forsythe was one they came up with. Adam seemed to associate her with some of the construction problems in town. Emma did some research and sent me this. They had gone to her. And they had asked Barnabas to look into her financials. Here's his report."

Bill took the papers, his eyes not leaving Andrew. "How did they come up with her?"

Andrew shrugged. "Adam said he had listed all the people in construction in town. Catriona picked up on her name, asked if she went to college, and made the connection to her brother that way. Stella was a partier even then."

Bill nodded as he read the lists. "Did they suspect all these people or just list them?"

"Just listed them from what Adam said. They were trying to figure out why Adam was attacked, why Carey had come back and what the group who approached Adam wanted."

"Whoa! Wait a moment! What group?" Bill leaned forward, setting the papers back on the deck.

"Just like the other guys. A group from town approached Adam and asked for his help." Andrew frowned as he went over his conversation with Adam. "He seemed to think he knew the third member of the group, the one who stayed in the background but he wouldn't give a name."

"That's interesting. I remember now. Adam did talk to me about that. When you said that, I wasn't sure if it had been another group." Bill stood as he saw Lily at the doorway, waving the warrants at him. "I can look more into her tomorrow. Right now, let me see if I can find Adam and Catriona."

"Keep me updated. I won't be going anywhere tonight, not with this paperwork."

Bill stood in the living room of the abandoned cabin, his eyes searching for evidence, even as the officers searched inside and outside of the derelict cabin.

"Bill, they were here. We have ropes with fresh cuts. Some blood in one of the rooms. Not a lot though." Lily turned around to talk to one of the officers, then followed him out of the cabin.

Bill stared around once more, then followed Lily to the edge of the lake.

"You think there was a boat here?"

"You can see where it was pulled up on the shore. There are two sets of tracks, one looking as if they were carrying something heavy." The officer shone his light around. "I don't see that the boat ever came back."

"That means we'll be looking at all the cabins along here then. And how many are there?" Bill sighed. "Let's get started the paperwork started, Lily."

She nodded. "I'll have the county boat head this way in the morning. There's not a lot we can do tonight."

"No, there isn't, except pray." Bill turned and watched her walk away, then looked out over the lake. Where are you two, he asked silently. Where did you disappear to? Are you even still alive?

His heart lifted in prayer. They needed to find these two and find them fast. He had learned to trust his instincts and those instincts were telling them Adam and Catriona didn't have long.

✧ ✧ ✧ ✧ ✧

The next morning, Andrew stood beside Bill, his eyes searching the land

208

around him and then the lake. Where are you two, he asked? We need to bring you home. His heart sank as he saw the police divers preparing to board the boat. Not this, please, Lord. Not this.

Bill was watching the divers. "I pray they're here for nothing, Andrew."

"I am too, Bill." He turned as he heard his name called and walked towards the officer heading his way. A few quick words and Andrew made his way up to the driveway and down it to where the road block was set up.

"Jonathan? How did you come to be here?"

Jonathan just shrugged. "Did you find them, Andrew? Are they safe?"

"We have evidence they were here, but they're not now. We're searching the cabins along the lake now, trying to find them."

Jonathan stared past him, catching a glimpse of one of the divers. He gave a low cry as his knees buckled. Andrew caught him before he hit the ground and gently set him down. He crouched beside him, his hand on his shoulder.

"No! They can't be!" Jonathan's cries turned to sobs and the officers turned away, their faces showing their emotions.

Andrew stayed by his friend's father, compassion on his face.

"Jonathan. We don't think they're in the lake. This is just a precaution. We have to search the lake just to make sure, until we find them. And we will find them." He spun on his heel, searching for the officer he wanted. "Here, let me have David take you home and stay with you. I promise to call you as soon as I have word."

Jonathan finally rose, nodding his head, wiping the tears from his face, his shoulders slumped. "How do I tell Hannah?"

"Let me call Silas for you and have him meet you. He'll find one of her friends to come stay with you." He watched as Jonathan finally agreed and then moved off with David, who kept a hand on Jonathan's arm.

Andrew turned to find Bill beside him.

"Is he okay?"

"I'm not sure, Bill. I just don't get how he was here."

"I don't either. Unless…." He shook his head. "Do you think he was told to come here?"

Andrew shot Bill a look. "That's entirely possible. Call David and have him find out." He turned back to face the lake. "How long have the divers been out there?"

"A couple of hours. They got started just before dawn. The group getting ready to go in are from Oak City. The county guys are just coming back out." He looked up as he heard a commotion at the shore and started to run that way, Andrew at his heels.

Lily turned as she heard them behind her. "They've found a body. The divers will have it up shortly."

"Male or female?" Andrew's heart was in his mouth. He was thankful that Jonathan had already left.

"They didn't say."

Thirty minutes later, Andrew watched as the medical examiner arrived. He took the wallet handed him. Nodding to the examiner, he opened the wallet, his hand freezing as he saw the name. He walked closer to the body, trying to see the face.

Bill appeared at his side, accepting the wallet from Andrew. "Carey? It's him. Then where are they?"

Andrew shook his head, taking the wallet back and handing it to the examiner. "We'll have to keep searching. How long do you think, Doc?"

"I would saw three to four days anyway. I'll know more once I've been able to do the examination."

Andre nodded and turned to walk away, his eyes narrowed as he searched the forest. "There's someone watching us, Bill. Have the teams searched the surrounding woods?"

"They're working through it now." Bill stopped. "I'm glad it wasn't them."

"You and me both. Just pray they aren't in there."

Bill nodded, then watched as Andrew walked away, his steps tired and slow, his shoulders slumped. He knew how Andrew felt. He felt the same way.

Late that afternoon, Bill tapped at Andrew's door and entered as he beckoned him in, sinking down gratefully and staring down at his runners. He would need to buy some new ones, he thought. These ones had been ruined today. He closed his eyes for a moment, trying to sort out his thoughts.

"Bill?" Andrew's soft voice caught at the edges of his thoughts as he started to drift to sleep.

He looked up, blinking to clear his eyes. "Andrew. They weren't in the lake. That much we know now."

Andrew nodded. "That's good. What about the cabins?"

"We working through them. The thing is some of the people are away and we can't get into them yet. Lily and a team are working at contacting them for permission to go in. I think she said there are about eight they haven't gotten to yet."

Andrew nodded, then looked down at his watch. "Go home, Bill. Catch some down time. Don't be here until 10 tomorrow morning."

"I will, if you will." Bill stood and stretched.

"I'm heading out as well. Phoebe said she's have a meal ready for me."

"She's really a special lady. She takes good care of you."

Andrew smiled as he thought of his wife. "She does. When I went into the bar that night and pulled her out, I never expected we'd be married or that I would be deeper in love with her each day." He watched as a look flickered across Bill's face. Lord, I don't know why he's never married, but You do. Provide that lady for him, please.

Chapter 16

_L_ittle did Adam and Catriona know what faced them the afternoon they walked out of the police department building. Adam ran after Catriona and pulled her to a stop, enveloping her in his arms.

"What a minute, okay?" He held her tight, not caring that people were staring at them.

"I am just so ticked off, Adam." Her posture was stiff. Then she relaxed against him, her arms going around him. "I just want this over."

"I know you do. But Andrew and his people are working as hard as they can." He reached for her hand. "We need to get back to your place. I can call a friend or a taxi or we can just walk."

"Let's walk, okay. Maybe it will clear our heads." She stared at him for a moment. "You didn't stay to talk to Andrew. I thought you would."

He shook his head. "No. You're the important one here. I needed to be with you and you needed me. That's what love is in my books, Catriona."

She sighed as they stared to walk away from the downtown area. "Where do we go from here then, Adam?"

"I don't know, love. Andrew's working on something, I know. He has the lists of names. Emma said she'd be talking with him." He pulled out his phone. "No messages yet from Emma." He stared up at the sky. "We both have work tomorrow, but on Saturday, let's head over to see your mother. Maybe she'll have an insight that we don't have."

"She might." Catriona's steps slowed as she approached her street. "I didn't realize it was such a long walk."

"It was a bit of one, wasn't it?" He pointed at her door. "Let's get something to drink and sit on the back deck before I take you out for dinner."

"Dinner, huh? What are we doing, dating or something?"

Her straight face and dry comment had Adam breaking out into laughter before he kissed her. "You know I love you deeply, don't you?"

She nodded, her eyes on his. "And I do you. Mom's been after me about wedding plans. I haven't had the heart to tell her we're waiting for now."

"And why are we waiting? Do we keep putting our life on hold for Carey and his friends?"

She stopped as she unlocked her door, turning to face him. "You are just so right, Adam. He's taken enough years from us. I'll get our lemonade and you pull out that calendar of yours. We'll set a date tonight and then call Silas."

That earned her another kiss and long hug. Adam turned as he heard footsteps behind her and frowned. He pulled her towards him and towards the door, thinking to get out and get to his truck.

He heard Catriona scream and turned back to see her struggling with her assailant, fighting to get away. Her purse and keys were on the floor, kicked aside in the struggle. Adam reached for her and found himself hitting the floor hard. He turned and kicked at his assailant, knocking him back through the door and off the porch. Adam threw himself through the door and onto his assailant. They fought, each trying to overcome the other, until Adam went limp. A third man had come up and stood, weapon in hand, having using the butt to knock Adam unconscious.

Catriona was held tight in her assailant's arms, her wrists now bound in front of her. Tears streaked her face as she stared at Adam's limp body. She didn't hear the words shouted at her, just felt herself pushed towards the truck parked behind Adam's. Shoved inside, she twisted to see where Adam was. His body was thrown in beside her before two of the men climbed in. She heard quiet words but they didn't register. She reached for Adam, her hands on his face, feeling for a pulse. He was alive, but battered. Lord, where are we going? Where are You? Couldn't You have prevented this?

She heard the sound of another truck, and shifted around to stare out the back window. She frowned. Now why would they be bringing Adam's truck?   She slumped back, her hands resting on Adam. She had no idea who their captors were, but she feared they wouldn't live to find out. She watched through the darkening sky as they drove around, aimlessly she thought. Finally one of the men pulled out his phone and then said something quietly to the other. He nodded and headed for the lake.   Her heart sank. This was it, she thought. We'll end up in the lake.   Tears filled her eyes against and she willed them back.   She wouldn't cry again, if she could help it.

She was dragged from the back of the truck and shoved into a rundown cabin and into one of the bedrooms, hitting the floor hard with her hands and knees. She stayed that way to catch her breath and gather her thoughts, looking up as Adam's body was dumped beside her. She turned as she heard the lock click in the door. Now what?

She turned Adam onto his back and reached for his bonds.   She couldn't get them loose.   She rolled him slightly to his side, hoping his penknife was still in his back pocket. She breathed a sigh of relief as she felt it, pushing it up until she could grasp him.   Using her teeth, she popped open a blade and reaching, slashed the ropes on both their wrists. She closed the knife and placed it on the floor. They would search her if she didn't and she shuddered at the thought of their hands on her.

Adam roused the next morning, groaning as he rolled over. His whole body hurt, but his face was the worst. He felt it, grimacing as he felt the bruises and cuts on it. He tried to raise his head, but the world was swirling around in front of his eyes. He heard soft movement and then a hand on his, drawing it back from his face.

"Adam? Can you hear me?" Catriona's voice was soft.

He nodded and regretted it. Squinting through one eye, he studied her. "You're okay?"

She nodded. "I am. Just some bruising on my wrists. What about you? You've been out all night."

"Help me sit up." He pushed at the floor and sank back down when his head spun.

"No. You need to rest, Adam." She shot a look at the door. "They've been in and out all night, checking on us."

"How many?"

"At least three. I think I heard a fourth voice but it was low enough I couldn't be sure." She stared down at him, her hand gently brushing at the dried blood. "I need some water to clean you up." She rose, searching the room but finding none. She sat back down beside him, pulling him close to her, her hand on his chest feeling it rise and fall as he slipped back into darkness.

Lost in her thoughts, she didn't hear the door open behind her or see the man standing there. Carey stood there, his eyes on his sister, a shuttered look in his eyes as he watched her sitting there, her eyes on Adam. Rage coursed through him. He was angry that they were together again. He thought he had changed that, made her promise not to see him. Then, he frowned. But then, she hadn't promised that after all, had she? She hadn't said a word that last day and then she had just walked away from where he had her locked up. Someone had left the door unlocked. He didn't realize it had been himself, that in the darkness of his drugs and alcohol, he had failed to lock the door that last day.

He stepped back, locking the door behind him and trying it to make sure it was locked. He wanted answers. He needed that notebook and codes that she had taken on him when she walked away. He had debts he had to pay and that was the only way he could see.

The two men with him looked up as he entered the kitchen, then shared a look. They had their orders. If Carey didn't have the material he promised in the next three or four days, he wouldn't be given another chance.

Late that afternoon, Adam felt himself dragged to his feet and to the kitchen. Catriona was already there, seated in a chair, her face showing her fear. Her eyes were on him, seeking help and peace, drawing from his strength.

Adam struggled to release himself from the grip he was held in, but the grip was too strong. He watched helplessly as one of the men approached Catriona, pulling her head back by her hair. She pulled away from him, her hand on her hair as she glared at him.

"Where is it?" His voice was coarse and hard.

"Where is what? I have no idea what you're talking about?"

Adam strained to reach her as her hand went to her mouth, wiping at the blood from the blow across her face. He couldn't get loose, no matter which way he turned or twisted.

An hour later, Adam caught his balance as he was shoved roughly into the bedroom, whirling to catch Catriona as she was flung into the room, wrapping her tight in his arms. Water bottles and sandwiches were dropped on the floor and the door slammed shut and the lock clicked.

He held her as she shuddered in shock, finally sinking to the floor and cradling her on his knee, his head on hers, as he prayed. Lord, what do they want? And how do we get out of here?

Four days later, Adam slumped to the floor. He had been beaten as well, trying to get to Catriona, to protect her. His eyes closed no matter how hard he tried to keep them open. When would it end, he wondered? How much more could she take before she broke completely?

He turned his head and then rolled reaching for her. His hand fell to the floor as darkness claimed him.

Catriona lay still, her hand cradled in the other, broken fingers lying crooked in the palm of her other hand. She had been beaten, fingers broken, all in an effort to find whatever it was that Carey had told them she had. She had been aware that day that Carey wasn't there, and that no one mentioned him at all. It had become a game to them, to try and break her physically as they tried to break her mentally.

The pain roused her and she sat up, lines grooved into her face as she cradled her hand to her ribs, ribs that were sore, bruised, cracked. It had made no difference to the men that she was a female. They delighted in bringing pain and suffering to her. Her blurry eyes stared around and she crawled towards the water bottle she saw, her fingers reaching for it, hitting it and sending it spinning away from her. She paused, head hanging down, as she drew a deep breath before sinking once more to the dirt-encrusted floor

The door opened and the men stood staring at the couple lying there, oblivious to them. A few words, a few nods, and the door was slammed shut and locked again. The men left, knowing that in doing so they had signed a death warrant for the two. They could get nothing from them. Adam knew nothing about what the material was. Catriona said she didn't and the men had begun to believe that she was telling the truth. Either way, it was too late. Even if she had told them, she and Adam would not be walking away from that shack.

Dust settled in the air over the cabin and surrounding brush and land. The ducks and loons called from the lake, the water lapping quietly at the shoreline. The birds began their singing once again as did the insects. The squirrels and chipmunks once more roamed the clearing, looking for food. The quiet settled down and death stared the two in the cabin in the face.

Two days later, the cabin door swung open, the movement causing the dust and dirt to swirl around the rooms. The young man stood in the doorway, looking behind him before moving silently forward. He searched the rooms, finally coming to the door that was locked. He fingered the lock and then stepped away, heading outside to find a large enough rock that would break the lock from the door. A few quick blows and the lock fell away. He pushed the door open, standing once more in silence and stillness searching the room. He dropped to his knees beside Catriona, then moved to Adam.

He dragged Adam to his feet and then over his shoulder, heading from the cabin with the heavy burden until he reached the motor boat he had pulled up on the shoreline. He gently laid Adam in the bottom of the boat, quickly assessing him, before he turned and stared back at the cabin, his mind trying to determine what had happened. He returned and swept Catriona into his arms, cradling her close as she cried out with pain.

Gently he laid her beside Adam, pulling a tarp over them to hide them. He had no idea who had done this to these two, but he was taking no chances that he would be stopped before he reached safety with them.

Wading out into the water, he pushed the boat out far enough he could safely lower the motor and clambered aboard, starting the motor and guiding the boat towards the far shore and a hidden cabin. He needed to get these two to medical personnel, but he wasn't sure who to trust.

He reached a rickety old dock and reached to tether the boat. Standing carefully he pulled back the tarp and reached to sweep Catriona into his arms again. He stepped across the deck to the cabin, shoving open the door and placing her on the floor. He returned to the boat and hauled Adam up and over his shoulder, returning to the cabin where he laid Adam down as well. He searched for blankets and pillows, finding some that he was surprised to find in good shape. Someone used this cabin, he thought, and recently.

Pallets on the floor, he moved each of them to one, covering them with a light blanket and tucking a pillow under their heads. He reached for a pail, heading out for water. He stared at the fireplace, then stared a small fire, heating what water he would need.

Late that night, Adam stirred, his eyes flickering open. He frowned as he stared around, sipping at the cup of water held to his mouth before he slipped back into the darkness.

The man stared at him from where he was kneeling at his side, then stared over at Catriona. Catriona had not moved, even when he set her fingers as best he could. He frowned as he thought about that, wondering who had done that and why. He felt along her jaw as well when he saw the bruising, uncertain of how to handle the broken jaw.

Two days passed as he tended to them, getting water and a broth he made from a rabbit he had snared down them. He sat back, deep in thought, on the second day. He needed to get them to help, but he really didn't want the men who had done this to find him or them. He had heard enough from Catriona's mumblings as she slept to know that their lives were in danger even now.

He turned as he heard the sound of a motorboat, walking outside and shutting the door behind him. He frowned as he watched it approach the dock, the police department insignia glowing in the mid-day sun. He walked forward, stopping to greet the officer who approached him.

The officer stared at him, then turned to his colleague in the boat, before heading after the man to the cabin. He stood for a moment staring at Catriona and Adam, then reached for his phone, then slid it away when he realized he had no service. A quiet quick discussion followed and then they carried the two down to the police boat, placing them carefully on the seats.

The officer jumped aboard, reaching for the tether as the man handed it to him.

"What's your name, so I can put it into the report?" The young officer stared up at the man standing there, golden hair reflecting the sun.

"Michael."

The officer looked down, then back up, staring around and standing back up on the dock. Where had Michael gone to? He was gone to quick to have made it back to the cabin or into the woods?

The two officers shared a look before they shrugged, heading across the lake to the marina.

Letting out a yell that caught the attention of everyone in the office, Bill slid his phone away as he ran to Andrew's office. Not finding him there, he searched the building, finally finding him in the break room. He stood for a moment, watching as Andrew leaned wearily against the counter, eyes closed, hands grasping the edge of the counter to keep himself upright, the scent of freshly-brewing coffee wafting through the air.

"Andrew?"

Bill's voice and its excited tone caused Andrew to turn, frowning. "Bill?   What's up?"

"We have them, Andrew.   Thad and Daniel are on their away across from the other side of the lake with them, heading for the town dock."

Andrew stared at him, his sleep-deprived mind taking a moment to understand the words. Then he was moving towards Bill. "Where do we need to be, at the dock or the hospital?"

"The hospital. I've sent someone for Jonathan and Hannah and given Emma a head's up as well. Abe was going to bring Catriona's mother this way when we had word."

"How are they?" Andrew slid behind the wheel of his car as Bill closed the passenger side door after himself.

"Unconscious. Thad said they've been beaten, Catriona more than Adam. I've had the paramedics waiting for them, and a team waiting at Emergency."

"Good. Any word on how they got there?"

"Thad didn't say or didn't know. He said that a man was with them." He frowned, then continued. "Thad said it was the strangest thing. Once they were in the boat, the man disappeared."

"Disappeared? How?"

Bill shrugged. "Thad wasn't real clear. We'll have to ask him when we see him."

Andrew strode rapidly in the Emergency Department, waving at the clerk, hesitating just long enough for the door to the examination rooms to open before he was through it looking for his officers, Bill on his heels.

"Thad?" Andrew stopped in front of the room, his gaze catching Daniel's eyes at at the next room.

"Andrew. The doctors are with them now. They said it would be a while."

"Any word on their condition?"

Thad shook his head. "It's too early yet for them to say. But you need to be aware they've both in rough shape. The paramedics said Catriona has a fractured jaw as well as some broken fingers on top of the other injuries. They didn't say much about Adam."

"Tell me how you found them."

"Daniel and I, well, we just decided we take the boat and go along the shoreline. We knew we had been to most of the cottages but there are some you don't see except from the water. This was one of them I knew we hadn't checked. The dock was in rough shape. When we pulled up to it, the man came from the cabin and met us. I went up with him when he said he had rescued them and brought them to that cabin. I still haven't figured out why he took them there, instead of bringing them into town. He didn't say, just avoided answering. We carried them down to the boat, I said something to him. When I looked back up, he was gone. Like in vanished. As if he had never been there." Andrew could tell Thad was bothered by that.

"An angel?"

Thad stared at him, eyes wide. "Really?" Then he shook his head. "I can't believe that for a moment." He turned his head as the door beside him opened.

"Andrew?" The Emergency Room physician reached to shake his hand. "Next of kin for Catriona?"

"That would be Adam. Then her mother. But her mother's on her way, just not present yet."

The doctor nodded, his eyes on the door to Adam's room. "I need to take her to surgery. She has a fractured jaw that needs to be repaired now. She also has some broken fingers that our plastic surgeon will be looking at during the surgery." He paused, trying to compose himself. "Her fingers, Andrew? It was deliberate, not an accident."

Andrew stared at him. "Torture, is what you're saying? Trying to get her to talk?"

The doctor nodded. "I've seen it before, in the larger cities, particularly with gangs." He paused for a moment. "We have someone else working on Adam. He'll be out shortly, I think." He headed for the nurses' station, as Andrew and Bill exchanged a glance.

"Thad, you go with her wherever she goes. She's in protective custody until we find the guys. I'll have someone relieve you at the end of your shift. Daniel, the same for you."

He pointed back towards the waiting room. "I'll be out there. If anything comes up, you come find me."

Hours later, Jonathan and Hannah looked up as the physician made his way to them, sinking wearily into a chair beside Hannah. The Emergency Department had been busy that day but his first priority had been Adam.

"Jonathan. Hannah. I understand Catriona is one of his next of kin now?" At their nod, he continued. "She's still in surgery, so I'm talking to you two. Adam is a lucky young man. He's taken some pretty bad beatings. Lots of bruising and cuts on his arms. It looks as if he really struggled to get away. He's dehydrated as well. I'll have a nurse come get you soon. We'll going to be transferring him up to a room on the medical floor. Once he's there, you can go in."

"Thank you, Doctor. Any word on Catriona?" Hannah voice was quiet.

He shook his head. "I haven't heard anything in the last hour or so, but they were working on her fingers the last I knew." At their shocked look, he sighed, his head going back as his eyes slid shut. "You didn't know?"

Jonathan spoke up. "Know what? We consider her a daughter to us. Her mother's on the way but not here yet."

"She had some fingers broken as well as her jaw."

Hannah's gasp of horror brought his attention to her face. "I'm sorry. I wish I didn't have to say that." He rose, his eyes on both of them. "I know you're praying folks. I've seen you around church. Both of these young people need your prayers. It's not just physical healing they'll need."

Jonathan stood to shake the physician's hand, then stared at Andrew before walking over to him.

"We need to talk, Andrew, without Hannah hearing us. I need to know what you've found out."

Andrew nodded, sighing to himself, wondering how he would ever explain it to Jonathan.

"Let's walk outside. Bill?" Bill nodded and watched the two men leave, standing to one side as a lady in a wheelchair came through the door.

Bill frowned, then recognized Matt from Abe's team. "Matt? This is Catriona's Mom?" Bill reached to shake their hands.

"Yes. This is Cara. Do you have word?"

Bill studied Cara, seeing her daughter in her face. "I do. She's in surgery right now. She has a fractured jaw and fingers they're working on. That on top of other injuries. Nothing major though." Bill pointed towards the chairs. "Sit there, Matt. I'll see if I can find out anything more for you."

Chapter 17

ndrew paced the hospital parking lot, Jonathan keeping step with him.

"What aren't you telling me, Andrew?" Jonathan's hand on his arm finally stopped him.

Andrew stared at his friend's father, a man he liked and respected, not quite sure how to proceed.

"You know what they say. Just spit it out. I don't need fancy words, just facts." Jonathan shoved his hands into his pockets. "He's here. He's alive. So is Catriona. That's what counts."

Andrew nodded. "I'm really not sure how to proceed, Jonathan. First, the body they found was Carey, Catriona's brother. Secondly, they were in that cabin but someone found them and moved them to safety. He looked after them for a couple of days from what I can gather." He stopped, his words choking him. "It looks as if

Catriona was beaten and tortured to make her talk. Adam's injuries are directly related to his trying to get to her and protect her."

Jonathan's eyes slid shut when Andrew finished, not realizing what the two had been through. "Tell me you have the ones who did this."

"Not yet. We need to talk to Catriona and Adam, and I'm not sure when that will be. We're running down leads now, following evidence. It's still a way to go yet."

Jonathan nodded as he turned to walk back to the hospital doors. "And you need to work through what you have. I understand." He was silent as he walked through the doors and sat beside Hannah, his hand going out to hold hers. Their eyes closed as they prayed.

Matt watched Adam's parents and then turned to Andrew, frowning as he saw the fatigue in him. He said a quiet word to Cara and then rose, walking towards Andrew.

"Andrew? What can we do to help?"

Andrew looked up as Matt spoke, nodding. "Thanks, Matt. For now, just stick with Cara. I have no idea where the next attack is going to happen. And it will happen."

"Abe's willing to send the rest of our guys if you need them."

Andrew nodded again. "Tell him no for now. Thank him for me. Excuse me." Andrew walked away to confer with Bill before heading back to his office. Where does it end, Lord, and how?

Adam stirred, his head turning restlessly on the pillow, his hands moving as if to try and fight off his captors. His eyes flickered open and then closed as he drifted off to sleep. The nurse standing beside him watched before turning to Hannah.

"He's sleeping now, Hannah. He'll likely sleep for a good while now. Can I get you anything?"

Hannah shook her head, pulling her chair closer. She held her son's hand, rubbing it with her other hand, staring at the bruising on his arms and face. Who could have done this?

Jonathan walked in a few minutes later, a cup of coffee in each hand. He reached to kiss Hannah before setting her coffee on the table.

"How is he?"

"He roused a few minutes ago. The nurse says he seems to be just sleeping now, which is good." She searched her husband's face, sensing something going on with him. "How's Catriona?"

"She's in recovery, from what Bill said. They're not letting anyone near her, not even her mother for now." He frowned as he turned to look at the door.

"What's bothering you, Jonathan? Something is." Hannah rubbed her husband's back.

"It's Cara. There's something not right there." He frowned again. "She doesn't act like someone who's been in a wheelchair for years. Do you know what I mean?"

Hannah nodded. "That's what bothering me, too. Have you talked to Bill or Andrew?"

He shook his head. "That's where I'm heading now.   Are you all right on your own?"

She stared at him. "Go. Take care of this."   She looked past him as the door cracked open. "There's Bill now. You don't have to go looking for him."

Bill frowned at the comment. "What did you need to talk to me about?"

"Catriona's mother. Did you look into her at all about what's been happening? She just doesn't seem right."   Jonathan's voice was hesitant. He hated to make a false accusation.

Bill stared at him, then at Hannah. "You two are serious, aren't you?"   He searched their faces. "You are! What made you think of that?"

Jonathan shrugged.   "Just something that doesn't seem right."

Bill nodded. "I'll call Lily and get her started on that.   First, though, how is Adam?"

"He's sleeping.   He was awake for a few minutes."   Hannah turned to her son, finding his eyes flickered as he tried to wake up. "I don't think he'll sleep long."

Andrew looked up as Bill walked into his office and sat, frowning at the interruption.

"I thought you were at the hospital."

Bill nodded. "Lily's there. I had to talk to you." He looked at his hands before he spoke. "I was asked if we investigated Cara."

"Cara? Catriona's mother? What? No, not that I know of. Why?"

"Hannah and Jonathan asked me if we had. He said she didn't act as if she belonged in a wheelchair. I sat and observed her for a while when she was on her own in the waiting room. I'm inclined to believe them. I asked our team to run an investigation." He handed over the folder he held. "This is the preliminary look. She's not a cripple, Andrew. Never has been. She's been playing every one of us, especially her daughter. I spoke with the investigator who looked at her husband's death. He's going back over that with a fine-tooth comb. He was never satisfied it was just an accident.”

Andrew sat back, hands scrubbing down his face. “This just gets better and better. Is she the one in charge of it all?”

Bill nodded. “That’s what we’re thinking. I’ve restricted all visitors to Catriona. No one but medical personnel get in and out. No family. No friends. Cara was not happy with that.” He turned to look at the door. “I also called Richard. His team is coming in to provide protection for those two until we wrap this up.”

“Good thinking.” Andrew flipped open the folder and began to read. “I don’t like this, Bill. I would say she’s been the one who had the information all along that Carey wanted. Do you suppose she ordered him killed?”

Bill sighed, his hands tightening in his lap. “That’s exactly what I think. I also think she was behind what happened to Catriona all those years ago. Matt said she seemed to want to control what was done for Catriona, not wanting anyone else to have a say. She didn’t like it when she was told she had no say, that Adam was the next of kin.

I've posted another officer at his door as well. She'll go after him."

Andrew stared at him. "You've really read her in this short of time." He pulled out his phone as it chimed. "It's Abe. Abe? What? Matt's at the hospital, yes. Who? Catriona? As far as I know she's still in recovery. Why? I see. Yes, we'll head there."

He rose as he pocketed his phone. "Abe's on his way. Ian's flying him over. Emma just uncovered the evidence we need about all those years ago and her husband's death. She's the one we've been looking for."

Catriona nodded, pain evident on her face, as the nurses shifted her from the stretcher to her bed, a soft groan drawn from her. She sipped from the straw in the glass of water and then laid her head back, her eyes closing. She was disoriented, not sure where she was other than she was in a hospital bed. Her eyes popped open as a hand touched her arm.

The surgeon stood there, his fingers on her pulse, then reaching to check the bandages on her fingers of her left hand.

"Catriona. You won't be able to speak very well, but we can understand you. Nod or shake your head if you have to. Now, you have three fingers we had to set the bones in. Thankfully, they were clean breaks and not too difficult to repair. Your jaw was fractured and we've had to wire it shut for now. You'll be about six weeks like this. It won't affect your job too much, I don't think.

"Now about the other issues of bruising and what not. They'll all heal in time. But if you need to talk to someone about all you've gone through, let the nurses know. We'll find someone for you. Any questions?"

She went to shake her head, then help up a finger. "Adam?"

"Adam? He's sleeping right now from what I understand. Bruising, some cuts. He wasn't hurt like you were, if that's what you're asking. Right now, I can't get him to see you. The police detective has vetoed any visitors for now and placed two police officers at your door. He's been awake, wanting to talk to you, but I've put him off for a day or so. If you need anything, push your buzzer. The nurses' station is right outside your door." He watched her for a couple of moments before walking away, stopping to speak to the nurses before heading for the locker room and home.

Catriona nodded, her eyes sliding shut. The pain was coming back, but she wasn't willing to take any medications. She didn't like the way it made her feel. If it got too bad, then she would. Her thoughts turned to Adam. Please, Lord, heal him. I don't know why You've let us go through, but You did. Heal us. Lead us to where You want us to work for You.

How much later, she wasn't sure, she awoke to soft movement in her room. She blinked to clear her eyes, searching for what had awakened her. She froze as she saw the figure standing over her.

"Mom?" Her voice was low. "That's not you. You can't walk."

Her mother gave a coarse laugh. "Of course, I can. I was never crippled. Just wanted to make you think I was, to keep you at home. Who do you think arranged for Carey to kidnap you and hide you away all those years ago? It wasn't his idea. Just like this wasn't his idea. Except the men got too forceful. They weren't supposed to hurt you. Now, you need to tell me where that book is. Carey's dead, so he can't tell me, even if he knew. You're the only one who does."

Catriona shook her head violently, pain wracking through her as she did so. "No. I don't know. I have never seen it." Her fingers pushed frantically at the buzzer but it wasn't working.

"No point calling for help because I already disconnected it. No one can hear you. You can't call for help." Her mother leaned over her, a gun held in her hand. "I'll kill you myself if you don't tell me what I want to know."

Catriona's eyes were fixed in horror on her mother, just barely seeing the form that slid in the door and crept up behind her. A quick movement, and Andrew had cuffs on Cara.

He dodged the kicks she sent his way, handing her over to the officer that was at the door. He searched the room, giving a quiet cry and dropping to his knees beside Bill, rolling his body over and feeling for a pulse. He searched and found the bullet hole in his shoulder, and sent out a cry for help. The room flooded with medical personnel, as they worked over Bill before lifting him to a stretcher and rushing him from the room.

Andrew then turned to Catriona, finding her sitting up in bed, horror on her face as she cupped her hands to her mouth. Her eyes rose to his.

Lily stood beside her, hand on her weapon, as Andrew approached.

"I think it's finally over, Catriona. Your mother was the one who was behind all this. We have some more investigating to do, but we'll be talking with both you and Adam in the next day or so. Right now, Lily's staying with you. A friend, Richard, is here with his security team. Silver and Naomi will be with you. The men will be with Adam. Richard will float between your two rooms. We're not letting you stay alone, not yet."

She nodded, her head going back, before she raised it again and clutched at Lily's hand.

"Adam?"

Lily nodded. "I'll go see how he is. There are officers at the door, so you'll be fine."

Catriona laid back once more, her eyes sliding shut as she slept.

Chapter 18

$\mathscr{A}$ week later, Andrew sat down in a chair at Adam's, a cup of coffee in his hand. Hannah had just fed them a roast beef dinner and he was full. He stared around at the ones gathered: Adam and Catriona, Jonathan and Hannah, Josiah and Faith. His heart hurt for Catriona as he watched her. Losing her brother to murder and then finding out it had been her mother all along was taking a toll on her, and she was struggling to cope. He knew she had been meeting with Silas for counselling and he was glad.

"First, Catriona. How are you feeling?" He laughed as she nodded, then grimaced. "About like that? Okay, so where do we start?

"First, we need to go back to your Dad, Catriona. The investigator took another look at his death. It was definitely an accident. No question there. Now, your mother. She was injured in that bad accident a number of years ago, became addicted to pain medication. When her doctor cut her off, she turned to the streets, becoming a dealer and working her way up the chain of command. She started Carey off on the drugs as well. Why, she won't say. She was behind his abduction of you all those years ago. She didn't want you out of her sight, thinking she could bring you into the drug trade as well. When that didn't work, she was livid when you moved away.

"She hired the men to harass and follow you both, hoping to drive a wedge between you again. When that didn't work, she stepped it up. Everything that happened to you, was done on her orders. She wanted a book she says you have, Catriona, that lists deals and monies received. Carey skimmed from her and hid it somewhere. That's what this has been about. We can't say for sure, but we think she ordered Carey's death. No one will deny or confirm it. The medical examiner did say it could have been an accident. He was high at the time that happened. Everything that happened to you, the window, the men following you, the thefts, the abduction of all you women, everything, that was your Mom.

"Now, Adam, your little group. I wish I knew who they were. They certainly pegged the situation. We've arrested Shelley Forsythe. For years, she has been selling substandard concrete. The town has building inspectors going over every building she was involved with. It will take time to sort that out.

"Now, I think that about covers it. Any questions? No. Good, because I have no more answers."

Quiet conversation broke out between them all. Adam sat with his arm around Catriona, watching her face.

"What's wrong, love?"

She shook her head. "I'm not sure, Adam. There's still something missing." It was hard for him to understand her words, as she tried to speak through her wired together jaw. She rose and headed for her office. He waited a moment, then followed.

He watched as she searched the shelves, touching various books before she frowned and pulled one down. She flipped it open and froze, then turned to him, holding it out.

He reached to take it from her, his eyes not leaving her face, seeing the devastation there. He looked down, seeing the names and numbers and dates.

"This is it? You've had it all along?"

"I did. I never knew that I did. I never looked at the books Carey would give me. His interests and mine were so different. When Andrew said something tonight, it made me wonder if I did have it."

He reached and drew her into a hug, arms tight around her. "You didn't know, love. I don't think it would have made any difference if you had given it up. You likely have been killed just because you looked at it."

He felt her nod against his chest, her hair brushing his chin. He felt the tears start and tightened his hold on her. He looked up as he heard quiet footsteps enter the room and then stop. He handed Andrew the book. Andrew took a look at it and then nodded, turning to leave. It was the last of the chain of evidence that he needed.

Adam felt the sorrow coursing through him. Why, Lord? Why did this have to happen? Then he felt peace flow through him, knowing that God had been there all along.

"Adam, who was Michael?" Catriona's quiet voice caught his attention.

"Michael? Oh, the man that found us? I have no idea."

"I think he was an angel sent by God to protect us. Why else would he have disappeared so quickly and completely."

"You may be right, love. You may be right. Come on. Let's get you some more of that good broth stuff, whatever it is you've been eating, and then spend some time with our family. Josiah has threatened to have Uncle Seth bring over their little guy."

"I'd like that. And we still need to set a date. I don't know if I can wait another five weeks until I get these wires off, though."

Adam gave a shout of laughter as he reached to kiss her thoroughly. Somehow, they managed even with her jaw wired shut.

The group in the living room turned as one when they heard Adam's laugh and then laughed themselves. Their family was back, was safe, and happy. That's all they could ask for, wasn't it? God had been gracious and good.

Epilogue

A year later, Catriona stood in the doorway to the spare room, studying the changes they had been making. They had been married for almost a year now, choosing to have a very quiet wedding with just their close friends and their family members that they wanted to be there. Her mother had not made it to trial, somehow finding a way to purchase drugs while awaiting trial and overdosing. The men under her had been tried and were now serving long prison terms.

She turned as Adam wrapped his arms around her, dropping a kiss on her mouth, then coming back for more. She finally pushed him away laughing.

"We're supposed to be working, hon."

"I know. But I just couldn't resist. Do you know how beautiful you are?"

"One of these days you might convince me. I love it when you tell me that. You've been my rock through all this. Now." She turned back to the room. "I think this will work."

He set his chin on her shoulder as he stared past her at the room, arms wrapped around her, feeling their child move. "Wow! It's beautiful. You must have hired an interior designer." He laughed as he ducked back from her elbow. "This is one lucky little kid, you know. I want to live in this room."

Catriona laughed. Their little one wasn't due for a couple of months, but she had put into place what she had planned for years for a nursery. Adam had said he didn't care what she did, gladly moving furniture, painting and building shelves and cupboards for her.

"It's ready, Adam. Now we have to wait." She chewed at her finger as he laughed at her. "I know. I was too impatient, wasn't I?"

"No. We'll just come in here everyday and pray for our little one, now that you've got it all set up."

She turned and arms around his neck hugged him, then drew him down for a kiss. "You always know the right thing to say. Thank you." She leaned back to look up at his face. "Through all of what we went through, I kept holding unto those promises of God, you know the ones where He promises protection and safety and peace. That's the only way I got through it. I had strayed away, but your example brought me back."

"Back to God and back to me. For a while there, I wasn't sure we'd even have a chance. I love you so much, Catriona."

Dear Readers

Thank you for picking up the story of Adam and Catriona. It was an interesting story to write. Once again, Adam and Catriona drove the plot line just by who they are and what they were facing and how God reached out to them.

Was there an angel in the story? Maybe, maybe not. I truly believe that God will provide us protection and help, and that He will use angels.

Remember that no matter what you're facing, big or small, God has promised never to leave us or forsake us. That's a promise you can count on.

God bless.

Ronna